Run From Darkness

Run From Darkness

Barbara Ann Philleo

Other Books By Barbara Ann Philleo

Other books by Barbara Ann Philleo

CANDLECURSE:

The Adventures of Molly Wiggins and Taco

MONSTER MOUNTAIN MYSTERY:

The Adventures of Molly Wiggins and Taco

PARTNERS IN CRIME:

The Adventures of Molly Wiggins and Taco

STICKS and STONES

THE HEAVEN CLUB

Callie and the Cult

Run From Darkness

Available on Amazon.com and where all books are sold

Chapter One

This was it – Sarah Jo Foster's last year of school! Even though it was home school, it was still school. Being finished – graduating – was a big deal. She knew her friends Abby Jacobs and Callie Morris were just as excited. For that matter, so were Wendy Granton and Laura Sanders who lived in faraway Addison where Sarah Jo had once lived. But now she was back in Pine Moor where life had begun for her. It would always be home no matter where she went. She called Abby to see about planning a get-together. Callie could be a part of it if she wanted too also.

"Hi Abby, what are you up to?"

"Not much, just fixing a sandwich."

"Really? Kinda early for lunch, isn't it?"

"I didn't have any breakfast."

"Hey Ab, I was just thinking about getting together and doing something. Got any ideas, that is if you can come over?"

"Wanna hang out at Connie's Cocoa Cottage for awhile?"

"Sure, I s'pose we could go there, It's a ways to walk but I need the exercise anyway," said Sarah Jo. "Should we ask Callie too?"

"Okay, I'll call her. For what time?"

"Let's make it for one-thirty."

"Okay, I'll be there for sure, and Callie too if she can make it. See ya."

***

1

The chalet-type ice cream establishment was nearly empty when Sarah Jo arrived. She noticed that Callie had been able to come and sat with Abby in a booth in the corner.

"Hi guys," greeted Sarah Jo. "Let me order something and I'll be right with you." She decided on a strawberry frozen yogurt sundae and took it back to the booth where her friends sat.

"Mmm, that looks good," commented Callie.

"So whatcha been up to?" asked Abby as she dipped her long spoon into a thick chocolate shake.

"Well, mainly setting up my schedule for my subjects."

"Is Latin one of them?" asked Callie.

"Yes, yes it is."

"Wow! You're a glutton for punishment, as my mom used to say."

"Why is that, Abby?" Sarah Jo dipped into her sundae and captured a strawberry. Connie didn't skimp on fruit in her frozen treats.

"Well, it's a tough subject for starters."

"It's a good, solid college course to take though and I wanted to make sure I got it in."

"Well, all I can say is good luck."

"Thanks for your vote of confidence, Abby," said Sarah Jo sarcastically.

"Hey, not to change the subject, but to change the subject..." snickered Callie, "it's already August; don't you think we should see if the Addison girls can come to a sleepover yet before school begins?"

"Good idea!" declared Sarah Jo. "Wendy and Laura haven't been here in months."

"I'll email them," said Callie. She finished off her swirl cone.

"Hey, how's Austin doing, Callie?" asked Abby.

"I guess he's okay. It hasn't been easy for him since he got out of that religious outfit he was in."

"But he's really done lots for the basketball team here, as you two probably know."

"Yeh, no kidding," said Sarah Jo. "My dad lets the rest of us know when he reads something about him in the paper. This year they should clinch the title. Last year they made it to the playoffs. Poor Austin sure had a weird situation."

"For sure!" exclaimed Sarah Jo. "It sure puts a whole new spin on religion – and parenting."

"Can you believe people actually buy into that stuff?" Abby had little tolerance for what she considered to be strange practices.

"Abby, I wouldn't have believed it if I hadn't seen it with my own eyes – and later researched it," said Callie. "Those people seemed very sincere, like they really believed the lies."

"Lies to you, Callie; truth to them," said Abby.

"You've got to be kidding," said Sarah Jo. "I mean they even have their own Bible – which really isn't even a Bible cuz it's written by some guy who is looked up to in their group."

"Well, to them it's truth, apparently," said Abby. "Look how entrenched Austin was in it."

"Well, because, he was brought up in it," reminded Callie. Abby, who implemented her straw in the now somewhat melted chocolate shake made sounds like she was nearing the bottom of the tall cup.

"Was it good, Abby?" asked Callie.

"Connie's shakes are always super good. They're going to have to roll me out of here." The girls laughed.

"Glad I stuck with a cone. Can't get into too much trouble with that, I guess," said Callie. "So what's this about having Wendy and Laura come to Pine Moor to get together with us?"

"Well, we just thought it would be nice for all of us to get together before school begins," said Abby. "Do a sleepover thing or something."

"We've done that before," said Sarah Jo. "How about we do something different?"

"Like what?" asked Callie. "Go on a cruise?"

"Hey," mock-scolded Sarah Jo, "why don't we do a campout at least for one night, that is if the weather's decent?"

"That's different for sure," said Abby.

"Right," chimed in Callie. "Ghost stories around the campfire and stuff like that."

"You know I don't believe in ghosts," replied Sarah Jo. "Evil spiritual creatures, yes; ghosts not so much."

"Aren't they the same?"

"No Callie," answered Sarah Jo. "Not the same. I mean I believe they can manifest themselves as what people call ghosts, but they're not the friendly kind like some people think they are."

"Hey, you guys are creeping me out. Enough with the ghost stuff," said Abby.

"Well, unless you actively seek them out, you're unlikely to encounter one," assured Sarah Jo. "As a child of God, that is."

"Hey, such serious talk here," said Connie as she swept up to their booth. "You ought to be having fun in these last few weeks before school. Just wondered if there was anything else I could get you." The girls shook their heads.

"Connie, can I ask you a question?" asked Callie. "Do you believe in ghosts?" Connie took a step back and looked shocked.

"Do I believe in *what* now?"

"Ghosts, you know....woooooo." Callie waved her arms.

"Wow! I've had customers ask me some strange questions like whether my ice cream comes from milk from guernsey or holstein cows, but never a question like this. Okay, let's see. Actually, I'm not sure. I've seen those ghost shows on TV, and they're pretty convincing."

"Yeh, but have *you* actually experienced anything like – weird or something?" Callie persisted. At that precise moment a customer entered the shop and Connie scurried off to the front of the store.

"I think she was about to tell us something weird," said Abby. "I'm glad she didn't get the chance."

"Well, that doesn't mean she still won't," replied Callie. "And if she does, you know you can count on it to be true."

"Well, there's no need to pursue it today," said Sarah Jo. "I think we should be thinking about our get-together with the girls from Addison."

"I think so too," said Abby. From that point on the discussion took on a lively tempo as they laughed their way through possible scenarios of their upcoming sleepover.

***

Sarah Jo would be hosting the campout/sleepover, and Callie would contact Wendy and Laura. Abby was responsible for assigning the various necessities such as food, drinks and the like. That evening at dinner Sarah Jo brought up the plan to her parents.

"That sounds like a great idea, honey," said Mom. "What would you like me to fix?"

"Oh, Abby's in charge of that. She'll let us know what each of us can bring. I do have another question though. Dad, do you think we can have a campfire in the back yard, like where we're camping out?"

"Sure, if you are willing to set up camp near the fire pit." Since the Fosters' yard was big, the girls could've wanted a campfire in a more remote area.

"Okay, as long as you don't let Mark snoop on us," replied Sarah Jo.

"Why would I want to snoop on a bunch of girls?" asked Mark incredulously.

"Cuz that's what little brothers do."

"I am *not* little!" declared Mark indignantly.

"Whatever." said Sarah Jo.

"Are you two about finished?" asked Mom. "We have enough ill will and arguing in the world without adding yours to it. You know I like dinnertime to be peaceful and positive."

"Yes, Mom," said the siblings in unison. The two cleared the table and Mom brought dessert in.

"What do we have here?" asked Dad, even though he could see for himself.

"Oh, it's just a little something I threw together," minimized Mom. It was plain to see that it was a peach shortcake, a summertime favorite. A large sweet biscuit cut in half and loaded with whatever fruit Mom had on hand and topped with billowy whipped cream.

"Works for me," said Mark, "*except* if you put lemon in there."

"Now why would I do that?" asked Mom. "Lemon is one fruit that only tastes good if it's sweetened – at least in a dessert."

"Your mom is so sweet that she doesn't need to use sugar with lemons," winked Dad.

"Dad-deee, pull...ease," whined Sarah Jo.

"I think that's sweet," said Mom. "Pun intended." They all laughed.

Chapter Two

Sarah Jo was surprised to get a call from Callie the next morning. She sounded out of breath and worried.

"What's wrong, Callie?" asked Sarah Jo.

"I just got a call from Austin. He wants to meet with me."

"Is it that cult outfit or are his parents giving him a hard time?"

"I have no idea. He just sounded kind of fired up about something."

"So, are you going to meet with him? That's what he wanted, right?" asked Sarah Jo.

"Yes. I told him I would. I sure hope this whole thing isn't a problem again."

"What do you mean?"

"Well, you know; that outfit he was in."

"I thought that was pretty cut and dried. I know he's living with foster parents – or *was* anyway."

"That's what I'm afraid of," said Callie. "It may be past tense – or will be."

"Well, he can't live with them forever. I thought it was just until he graduated."

"I know, but I sure would hate to see him get tangled up with those people again."

"Who – his parents?"

"No silly, that cult outfit he was in."

"Well, Austin is almost an adult. He's got to grow up sometime. And if it *were* so maybe he's meant to witness to them," said Sarah Jo. "By the way, did you contact Wendy and Laura yet?"

"Haven't had a chance to, but I will."

"Okay, well let me know as soon as possible. We need to get these plans in place sooner rather than later. Plus, I'll be curious to know about Austin."

"Yeh, me too, Sarah Jo. Well, gotta run. Talk to you later. Bye!"

***

Sarah Jo wondered what Callie's meeting with Austin would turn out to be about, but she couldn't waste her day thinking about it. Mom had asked her to pick tomatoes from the garden so that she could can them later when she got back from shopping. She'd said that she needed more canning supplies because the garden this year was yielding bumper crops of just about everything. It was true for sure where the tomatoes were concerned. Large red dots of color covered the plants from top to bottom. By the time Sarah Jo had finished, she had three quarters of a bushel of tomatoes, and those were the ones that were ready. Many more promised to ripen fully within the next few days.

She wiped beads of sweat off her brow with the bottom of her shirt. This was better exercise than going to a gym like people paid for. Plus, this was her way of contributing to the family. Her parents had done a lot for her and she was grateful. Not all kids had it as good as she did. She lugged the basket to the house and put it in the shade. As she turned to go, she thought better of it and snatched a plump juicy tomato from the top. The bite she took yielded flavorful juices that dripped down her chin. It tasted good now, and the tomatoes would taste good in the middle of winter in the form of spaghetti sauce too.

"Hey," said Mark as he flew into the driveway on his bike. "What's that?"

"What's *what?* This tomato? Go ahead, you can take one too."

"Really – can I?"

"Yes Mark, you really can."

"And it's all mine?" asked Mark as he picked out a choice tomato.

"Yes Mark, it's all yours. Why are you asking such idiotic questions?"

"This is why." He took the tomato and smacked it hard against the old maple tree near the garage.

"Marrrrk – you jerk! Why did you do that? I would've eaten it." The tomato's juice ran down the rough bark of the tree while the pulp remained as a splatter on it.

"Because, I needed pitching practice, that's why. Something you wouldn't understand." Mom pulled up in the van.

"Hey, I could use some help here," said Mom as she got out.

"Better not count on Mark for that. He might pitch the groceries at something because he needs practice – or so he says."

"I must have missed something here," mumbled Mom as she pulled a box of canning jars out of the back of the van for Mark to carry. Sarah Jo made a disgusted face and took a box as well.

"You look like you just ate a really sour dill pickle," said Mom to Sarah Jo as she carried the last box herself.

"If I did it was cuz Mark didn't get to it first." Mom just shook her head.

***

Dinner was interesting that night, at least to Sarah Jo's way of thinking, because somehow the conversation shifted back to tomatoes. Dad had given his full approval of the quarts of tomatoes Mom had just canned cooling on a towel on the counter.

"Reminds me of an old joke I heard a long time ago. A salesman had stopped by a farmer's house and was looking at the garden bounty and--"

"Bounty?" Mark cut in.

Vegetables, brainiac," said Sarah Jo."

"Oh..."

So anyway," resumed Dad, "the salesman asked the farmer what he did with all those vegetables. The farmer said, 'We eat what we can, and what we can't, we can'."

"Huh?" asked Mark.

"That's corny," said Sarah Jo as she giggled at her own joke. There was a twinkle in Dad's eye, knowing that he'd made his son think about what he said. No one explained it to him and the moment was interrupted by the phone ringing. Sarah Jo answered. It was Callie.

"What's up?"

"Sarah Jo, you aren't going to believe this. I saw Austin earlier. Now I know why he wanted to see me."

"Bad news?"

"No, not to my way of thinking."

"Spill, Callie, spill." When Sarah Jo noticed the family looking in her direction, she decided to go out on the deck with the cordless. "So what did Austin say? Was it about that cult outfit?"

"Hey, slow down! You're going sixty miles an hour in a thirty mile an hour zone."

"Sorry Cal, just curious is all."

"Okay, here's the deal. Austin asked me to the Homecoming dance."

"Really? What did you tell him?"

"Nothing yet."

"Cal, you must've said *something*. You can't not just answer someone who's asked you a question like that."

"I told him I would get back to him, that he caught me off guard. I wanted to talk to my parents about it first."

"Did you?"

"Yes, I did. They said it was okay if we went in a group with others."

"Isn't that what the kids usually do?" asked Sarah Jo.

"No, there are a lot of them that just go as couples," replied Callie. "It's sort of stupid because it's just too easy for things to get too serious. I mean what do you talk to one person about for a whole evening."

"Yeh, I see your point. So who do you think will all go in your group?"

"That's the good part. If Austin knows that's the only way I can go, it kind of puts some responsibility on him to come up with some names of couples."

"Makes sense to me."

"By the way, I did reach Wendy and she said she'd call Laura about coming here. She checked with her mother and she said it would be okay, if her dad went along with it, which he did. So now there's just Laura, and Wendy said she'd call as soon as she knew if Laura could make it."

"Great," said Sarah Jo. "We should do it as soon as possible because it'll depend on the weather. If we get a good forecast this next week we can do it then, don't you think?"

"Uh yeh, actually I *do* think – at least once in awhile."

"Callie, now you're being silly. You know what I meant."

"Yeh, I do, and I'll call you just as soon as I hear from Wendy."

*****

As it turned out, Laura could make it and the weather held out on Thursday when they ended up getting together. The girls laughed and kidded one another as they set up their lodging for that night. Sarah Jo's parents had invested in a good tent the year before. It turned out to be perfect shelter for the girls. They got the campfire that they'd asked for but only on the condition that they had the hose nearby - Dad's orders. That was okay; one could never be too careful. So as twilight dimmed the landscape, a cheerful fire crackled in the fire pit.

"I sure feel bad that Abby had to back out at the last minute," said Sarah Jo. "She was coughing when she told me. Her mother told her she felt the night air would just be too much for her. I guess she had bronchitis when she was younger and her mother didn't want to take any chances." They all agreed that it was a great loss that she couldn't be there.

Chapter Three

"So, what's been happening with you two since we last got together?" asked Sarah Jo as she crossed her legs and sat down on the old plaid stadium blanket used for camping.

"My brother Frankie has decided he wants to be a changed man. No more smoking or drinking or drugs," volunteered Laura.

"Really?" asked Callie.

"Wow!" exclaimed Sarah Jo.

"That's so cool," said Wendy as she draped her zippered hoodie around her shoulders.

"Yeh, I think so too," agreed Laura.

"Girls, did you get enough to eat?" called Mrs. Foster from the deck.

"Yes," they replied in unison with nods.

"Ready for marshmallows?"

"Yes Mom," answered Sarah Jo. "Do we still have our skewer things, like you use for shish kebabs?"

"I'll bring them out with the marshmallows, dear." When she returned, she was accompanied by a tall figure belonging to none other than Austin Reynolds.

"Hi, guess my timing was all off – or maybe it was just right," he said affably. "Callie said you were having a campfire tonight. I hope you don't mind that I sorta invited myself. I'll leave if you want."

"You'll do no such thing!" said Mrs. Foster emphatically. "At least have a few marshmallows with the girls."

"Are you sure you don't mind?" he asked the girls. No one objected, so Austin sat on the large backpack he had with him.

"Hey, if your laptop is in there, it's going to morph into a pancake," remarked Laura. The girls chuckled.

"Not to worry," he assured them. "What I have will add some excitement to your night."

"Hey, what's in there – a board game?" asked Sarah Jo.

"Well sorta. I think it's kind of fun, but it's more fun when someone else plays too. And an audience can never hurt." Sarah Jo's mother came back out to where the group was sitting around the fire pit.

"It looks like everyone's having fun here, but I just want to tell you that it's eight-thirty. Austin you'll need to leave in an hour."

"Yes ma'am." Mrs. Foster crossed the yard and went back into the house.

"So Austin, just what *is* in that backpack of yours?" asked Callie. Austin lifted himself up and pulled out the backpack.

"Watch and be impressed, ladies." He pulled out a box that contained a board. In the middle was a spinner and all around the board were letters and numbers. He placed it on the grass in front of him.

"What is that?" asked Sarah Jo as she moved closer to get a better look.

"It's called Spin and Win – or Not!"

"Huh?" said Laura. "What does *that* mean?"

"Well, each person spins the spinner until a word is spelled out." explained Austin. "Each person continues until a phrase or sentence is made. When it is, that is meant for the person who spun first. Then the second person goes."

"Doesn't make much sense to me," said Wendy. "But what do I know? I've never even heard of the game before."

"Let's try it," suggested Austin. "Who wants to go first?"

"I guess I'll go," volunteered Laura. She gave the spinner a spin. It pointed to the *y*. Then Callie spun and came up with an *o*. Sarah Jo spun a *u*.

"Hey, it spells 'you'," said Wendy. "Let me spin. Maybe it was just coincidence." The next letter was an *r*.

"Hmmm," said Austin. "I wonder what that means."

"Probably nothing," said Callie.

"I didn't spin yet. Let me try," said Austin. The spin yielded an *s*. "Okay, so it says 'yours'."

"This is wacky," declared Laura. "What's it sposed to mean?"

"Well, if it doesn't make sense, we should keep spinning till it does," said Austin. They all took another run at spinning and produced *bewar*.

"Now that *is* wacky," said Callie.

"Wait," said Austin. Let me take one last spin." He did and the pointer stopped at the *e* followed by a *4*.

"That completes another word," said Callie. "I'd say that's it. But how does it apply to Laura?"

"It's all just for fun, Cal. Don't take it so seriously," said Sarah Jo.

"Wait! Let me go next," said Callie. She spun and the pointer stopped at *n*. Sarah Jo spun and came up with an *o*. Wendy spun a *t*.

"Not?" said Laura. "Let me spin and see what comes next. The letter she landed on was *y*.

"We're probably out of order here, but I'm going to spin next anyway. We know Callie spun first this time so this message is for her. Austin spun an *o*. Sarah Jo spun a u.

"Let's see what letter comes up next," said Laura. "We're not in order anyway, so I'll spin. I don't think it matters as long as you remember who did the first spin." Laura's spin produced the number five. They all laughed.

"Well, I guess it was finished," said Austin. "It spelled out *not you5*".

"That doesn't make sense," said Callie.

"To me either," said Sarah Jo. "Let's quit while we're ahead."

"Hey," declared Austin, "I've gotta hit the trail. I need to be able to see." He folded the board and put it in his backpack.

"Did you walk?" asked Callie.

"No, he flew in his personal jet," said Wendy, giggling.

"Yeh right!" said Austin. "No, I rode my bike. Hey Cal, can you walk over to my bike with me?"

"Sure," said Callie and leapt to her feet. Sarah Jo figured it had to do with his question about going to the Homecoming dance with him.

***

After Austin left, the girls got into their "serious talk," as Callie put it. It would probably keep them up half the night like it usually did. Eventually, they got into the "juicy stuff" like Austin asking Callie to go to the Homecoming dance.

"What are you going to wear?" asked Laura.

"I don't know yet. It'll probably be kind of cold out, so something with at least short or three-quarter length sleeves."

"Or you could wear sleeveless and bring a wrap," said Wendy.

"Well, it's not exactly the Prom," replied Callie. "Besides, I don't want to get all dressed up if Austin is dressed more casually. I guess it doesn't matter cuz Mom has the final say."

"You'll really be the belle of the ball," said Wendy as she cuddled into the old quilt wrapped around her shoulders.

"The *what* of the *what?*" asked Callie.

"Oh, that's an old saying my grandma said once," replied Wendy.

"Hey, before I forget," said Sarah Jo, "how are your projects going there in Addison? Remember our good works projects we talked about last time?"

"They might be good works, but they won't get me into heaven," said Laura. "I learned that at a Heaven Club meeting."

"That's kind of weird, isn't it? I mean if you don't need to do good works to get into heaven, then why do them?"

"Wendy, you're kidding me, right?" said Sarah Jo. "I mean there are a lot of people who do good works but if they don't believe the gospel message and have faith in Jesus as the only one who can save them, what good does it do?"

"A lot probably if you're a starving little kid from Africa," said Laura.

"Well, that's true," said Callie. "But in order to get into heaven it's not just about feeding the hungry, but it *is* part of what we should be doing"

"Okay, I think I told you guys, getting back to the projects part, that I have been working on my brother and I do think he's really seeing the error of his ways," said Laura.

"That's great," said Sarah Jo as she poked the fire with a stick. "What about you, Wendy? How's your babysitting coming along?"

"Actually, really well. Mrs. Elkins really likes me mainly cuz Heather does. She'd probably do anything for her daughter. Anyway, she recommended me to her friends to babysit their kids."

"Wow!" said Callie. "Sounds like you've really got a babysitting service there." The light of the flames danced on Wendy's smiling face as she nodded.

"Yes, and Callie and I have been going to our local nursing home to read to the residents there as well as to work through the Commission on Seniors to help them in their homes," said Sarah Jo. "You have to get certified for that, but it's been a great way to serve."

"Well, it sounds like we all have our marching orders as my dad calls it," said Callie. "I guess we really can make a difference in our communities."

"I spose we should call it a night and hit the sleeping bags," said Sarah Jo. "Let's take some of this extra food inside first." Upon their return, they traded light from the fire for flashlights. The cool night air was motivation to crawl into their sleeping bags, ending up like caterpillars in their cocoons. Of course, that didn't stop their conversation which carried on into the wee hours. One by one the voices diminished until the night air was silent except for an owl hooting in the distance.

***

Morning dawned bright – and early – to the girls' way of thinking. They all woke up at nearly the same time because Mark's voice called out from the back door to announce breakfast.

"Come and get it, ladies! All sluggards will go hungry! Waffles are on the menu!"

"Sluggards?" mumbled Laura sleepily. "What's a sluggard?"

"Oh, don't pay any attention to my dumb brother. He just wanted to be annoying and get his jabs in. I had a feeling he wouldn't be able to resist."

"Well, he got a good one in, Sarah Jo. We're awake now," said Callie. Wendy stirred in her sleeping bag as well.

"I spose we might as well get up now," sighed Sarah Jo.

"*What* – and give your brother the satisfaction?" asked Callie. She scrunched farther down in her sleeping bag.

"Okay then, whoever wants to can get up," said Sarah Jo. "I know I won't be able to get back to sleep again."

"Oh, all right! You win – or shall I say Mark wins," retorted Callie.

"Hey, I have to admit that my brother can be a pain sometimes, but he does whip up a mean batch of waffles."

"That's what I'm afraid of," muttered Callie. One by one the girls entered the house and were rewarded with the smell of freshly made waffles.

"Well, it's about time," declared Mark who wielded a spatula. "I thought I'd have to eat these all by myself. Well, except for Mom and Dad." The girls sat down at the table. Mark served each of the girls individually. He carefully set a plate before Callie then picked it up again.

"These are for Laura, not you."

"Well, excuse *me!*" said Callie. "Maybe I should just go for toast this morning."

"Mark, do you know the meaning of *rude?*" asked Sarah Jo. "When I say 'Oh brother!' do I mean it!"

"Very funny, sis." The girls dug into their waffles and were enjoying them with one exception – Laura who grimaced as she took her first bite.

"Where did you learn to cook, Mark? This waffle is terrible! You must've mistaken teaspoon for tablespoon when it came to salt."

"There's nothing wrong with mine," said Callie.

"Mine either," said Wendy. "They're pretty good."

"Let me taste yours, Laura," said Sarah Jo. She reached over and took a forkful to her mouth and frowned. "Yecch! Mark, what did you do to her waffle?" She spit the waffle out into her napkin.

"What are you talking about? They're all from the same batter." Mark had a look of exaggerated innocence on his face.

"That's it! I'm calling Mom and Dad down." Sarah Jo's mouth opened wide, poised at yelling.

"No don't – guilty as charged. I just wanted to have a little fun. What's wrong with that?"

"Nothing if *you're* the one eating a salty waffle. Now you apologize right now – or I'll tell Mom and Dad. And make her a good waffle – now!"

"Sorrrry," said Mark, looking down at his shoes mock ashamedly.

"Mark!"

"Hey, I said I was sorry." He replaced the bad waffle with a new one.

"What's all the commotion down here," said Dad. "Ah, I see Mark is being a servant today. Why all the noise?"

"Ask *him*," said Sarah Jo. Mark mumbled something unintelligible.

"I don't know what you're stammering about, son, but make me some waffles. Your mother will be down soon."

"Yes sir."

***

The girls went back to the tent and rolled their sleeping bags. Everything else was put into their backpacks, except for the blankets and quilts they'd used the night before which they spread out on the grass and sat on. Wendy and Laura talked about mission trips their church had planned to inner city areas.

"Isn't it sort of scary going to those places?" asked Callie.

"No, not really," answered Wendy. "There are hurting people everywhere. They're thankful for the help."

"So what do you do exactly?"

"Well Callie, pretty much what we do on most mission trips – feed them physically *and* spiritually. They are grateful for both. The food feeds their bodies, but the spiritual gives them hope."

"Sounds pretty basic," said Callie.

"So, how's the Heaven Club doing there in Addison?" asked Sarah Jo as she went from sitting to lying on her side while propping her head in one hand.

"It's going great," replied Wendy. "It's grown a lot."

"That's great news," said Callie.

"You know," said Laura, "it's kind of strange some of the questions newcomers have asked."

"Like what?" asked Sarah Jo.

"Well, it's like one lady asked about her cousin who had died about a year ago. She said someone at the funeral had said that the cousin is up in heaven making pies because she always took first place at the fair with them."

"So, what's wrong with that, Laura?"

"Only that she didn't know Jesus, according to what this lady said. She said she had wanted to share the gospel with her cousin, but her cousin would have none of it."

"And...?"

"Callie! You know the answer to that. Pastor had to tell her the truth. I could see it wasn't easy but he wasn't going to lie."

"Laura, unfortunately, it is true. He can't go against what the Bible clearly teaches just because a loved one made a wrong choice," said Sarah Jo. "Doesn't it say there's only one way to God, and that's through Jesus Christ?"

"Well yeh, but the lady looked so sad when Pastor told her the truth."

"What's sad is that her cousin didn't listen to her when she had the chance, Laura," said Sarah Jo.

"Maybe she was too busy making prize-winning pies," commented Wendy.

"Uhh, or fifty billion other things that people use as excuses to avoid the issue of their own mortality," said Callie.

"Wow! That's a ten dollar word, as my grandma would say," said Wendy.

"Hey, let's switch the subject," said Laura. "Let's talk about something else."

"How about something weird?" suggested Wendy. "This morning while I was still in my sleeping bag after you guys left to go eat breakfast, I thought of those messages or whatever you want to call them, that came from that game last night."

"Yeh, so?" asked Callie.

"Well, I just thought it was weird what happened this morning at breakfast."

"In what way, Wendy?"

"Remember the messages? One was 'yours beware' and the other was 'not you'."

"So, what is that supposed to mean?" persisted Callie.

"The one having to do with Laura was 'yours beware'," said Wendy. "The one for you was 'not you'."

"So?" asked Sarah Jo and Callie in unison.

"Well, look who got the salty waffle – it was Laura. But Callie didn't," said Wendy.

"For that matter, none of us others did either."

"Sarah Jo, don't you see my point?" said Wendy. "It was like those messages from the game were a prediction."

"Prediction?" repeated Sarah Jo. "I'd say it was more like a co-incidence."

"Not exactly," Laura chimed in. "It was like a moronic joke."

"Still," said Wendy, "it was just plain weird to be so spot on."

Chapter Four

It had already been a week since the girls' overnight and Sarah Jo missed them. She told Abby about what had gone on and about Austin's visit that night around the campfire.

"Well, I'm glad I wasn't there then. That sounds a little bit freaky what happened with that game."

"It's just a game, Abby, for heaven's sake!"

"I know, but what you say happened at breakfast was weird enough. The only thing that sounded about right was your brother pulling that trick on Laura."

"She took it in good spirits though," assured Sarah Jo.

"As opposed to what – *bad* spirits?"

"Let's drop it. You know, we talked make-up and stuff. We think you've been wearing the wrong color for your skin type.

"Are you kidding me?" asked Abby incredulously. "Who are you guys to criticize?"

"Just trying to be helpful."

"Pleeease, sometime tell me when you have a split second," retorted Abby. The conversation transitioned into school topics and it was a subject they both enjoyed talking about; that, and the future. Later, Callie called Sarah Jo about her Homecoming plans with Austin. She wondered if Sarah Jo had been invited by anyone.

"No, not yet and I doubt if I will, Callie."

"Why do you say that?"

"Cuz I don't know that many guys from school. Why would they ask me?" asked Sarah Jo as she stretched out on the sofa.

"Well, it's not exactly like you're chopped liver. Let me ask Austin if someone on the team--"

"Don't you dare, Callie!"

"Umm... I'm afraid it's too late for that, Sarah Jo. He already asked me if he could do that, and I said 'why not?' seeing as how the worst you could do is say no."

"Callie! How could you? How could Austin?"

"Hey, there's worse things. Just think, you and I could go to the dance together with our dates."

"Dates – hmmph! I think you just set this up so your parents would let you go since they wouldn't let the two of you go by yourselves."

"Wrong!"

***

It didn't take long to find out who Austin had chosen as a date for Sarah Jo. She got a call right after dinner from a Luke Holman, a very tall sandy haired guy who played center on the team. The conversation was awkward at first, but later became more relaxed as Luke tried to put her at ease.

"Listen, Sarah Jo; Austin set this whole thing up. I was a little uncomfortable about it because I didn't know you and I figured you might just scrap the idea when I called."

"How do you know that I still won't?"

"Well, Austin said you were a super nice person and I believe him."

"Do you believe everything you hear?"

"When it comes from Austin, yes." The two continued small talk for awhile, then Luke blurted out, "So, will you do the honor of accompanying me to the dance?"

"I'll need to talk to my parents about it first, just like Callie did. I'll let you know."

"Do you have my number?"

"I do now," answered Sarah Jo. After she'd hung up she thought about Luke's invitation. She *did* need to get out more, but she definitely wasn't interested in dating. She knew most of the regular school kids did that and she thought it was a mistake. Some kids were going on dates as young as thirteen and some probably even younger. It was too much fun being a kid – even an older one – to throw it away on another person. Guys had a way of getting your attention drawn to themselves and for right now she wanted to focus on herself and the career she'd chosen. There would be plenty of time for dating when she was a bit older, once she'd gotten a good foundation in her training for her life's work.

"Hey squirt, whatcha doing?" asked Sarah Jo of her younger brother as he came to the door of her bedroom. He looked a bit perplexed.

"Promise you won't laugh?"

"I can't promise *that*," said Sarah Jo. "I'll try not to though."

"Well, I know it sounds sorta goofy but I'd like to try out for the team this year."

"What team?"

"You know, the home school group has a basketball team – well, other teams too – and we play other cities in our part of the state." Mark came in and perched on the edge of her desk.

"So, you're saying you want to be on the home school basketball team?" repeated Sarah Jo.

"Cut it out, Sarah Jo. You know that's what I just said."

"Hey, cool it, Mark. Just making sure I heard you right."

"I know, it's crazy, isn't it? Wanting to be a basketball player and all."

"What brought on this sudden interest in playing basketball?"

"Why do I have to have a reason? I want to cuz I want to."

"Well, it's just that most people have a reason for what they want to do," said Sarah Jo.

"Isn't wanting to reason enough?"

"I suppose it is. Have you told Mom and Dad yet?"

"Not yet, but I think I will at dinner tonight."

"Hey buddy, why don't you first go and pray about it. See what it is that God wants for you."

"You and your prayer, Sarah Jo. Don't you ever think about other stuff besides God?"

"Has God been good to you?" Mark dragged one foot across the floor as if in deep thought.

"Yeh, I guess so," he replied.

"Well, why would God let you down now?" Mark's face brightened.

"Yeh, why would God do that?"

***

That night at dinner, the conversation was lively. Dad had a good day and so did Mom. Dinner was stew – and it was good! Sarah Jo went for seconds.

"Dad, Mom, I have something to tell you," said Mark as he laid his fork down.

"What would that be, son?" asked Dad.

"Well, you know how you're always telling me to get off the couch and do stuff?"

"Yes, and I can think of a long list of things," said Mom.

"Not *that* kind of stuff!"

"Easy now, Mark," cautioned Dad. "Just what is it you're talking about?"

"I want to try out for the basketball team. You know, the home school group's team."

"Yes, I know what you're talking about, son."

"Well, I'd like to try out for it."

"Do you understand the responsibilities that go with that, Mark?" asked Dad. "Basketball practice isn't optional. You'll have to keep up your studies too."

"I know, Dad. I've thought about all that."

"Plus, you'll have to keep up your chores," said Mom. Mark grimaced.

"I know," he answered less than enthusiastically. "I will."

"When is your first practice, son?"

"In a couple weeks."

"Well, we'll discuss this more, but for right now finish your dinner. You'll have to eat well to maintain your body for an active sport like that, Mark."

"Yes sir!" said Mark, taking that to be the green light to his request. He loaded his plate with more of everything – even broccoli.

"So Sarah Jo, what's going on with you?" asked Mom.

"Well, I guess there's no need to hold off on saying anything any longer. Callie and Austin want me to go to the Homecoming dance with them and Austin's friend Luke. He's on the basketball team with Austin."

"Does he have a last name?" asked Dad jokingly.

"Daaad, of course. Doesn't everybody? His last name is Holman."

"Holman," repeated Dad. "Would that be Holman of Holman's Hardware?"

"Beats me," said Sarah Jo.

"I believe it could be. Holman's Hardware has been run by the Holman family for years. I guess every one's been guaranteed a job there because they're mostly family members," said Dad. "Good store too. I can find practically everything I need there."

"So, do you want to go with him, Sarah Jo?" asked Mom as she passed the broccoli around one more time.

"I guess so," came the weak reply. "I mean it's not like I've been waiting by the phone for someone to ask me." Mark chuckled.

"That would be a long wait," he said.

"Mark!" Dad shot him a warning glance.

"Well, right now I've been thinking more about school than my social life," said Sarah Jo.

"As it should be, dear," said Mom. "This is a very important time in your life." She got up from the table to bring back a plate of chocolate chip cookies. "Anyone for dessert?"

"There's nothing wrong with going to a dance at your age, Sarah Jo. In fact, it might be nice for you to get out," said Dad as he took a cookie. "It's just that dating is emphasized way too much these days. I think parents should have stronger guidelines for their kids."

"I didn't say I wanted to go, but I will if you and Mom have no problem with that."

"What is it that *you* want, Sarah Jo?"

"I'm okay with it, Mom. I'll probably have fun. I'm not the greatest dancer, but Luke probably isn't either."

"Well, if he's on the basketball team he may be better than you think," joked Dad.

"Then I guess I'll have to try and keep up with him," said Sarah Jo hopefully.

***

Sarah Jo was awakened in the middle of the night by an ear splitting clap of thunder. It startled her out of a deep sleep. She heard Mom and Dad talking in their room, and Mark running down the hall.

"What happened?" asked Mark as he stopped by his parents' door.

"I don't know. Thunder for sure, but lightning could've struck that old oak tree in the yard. I'll check from the porch. Where is that flashlight with the extra bright beam?"

"I left it on the hall table," said Mom. "That way if the lights go out we have it handy up here."

"Hey, what's going on?" asked Sarah Jo.

"I'm not sure," said Dad. "Lightning must've struck nearby. I'm going to check the yard from the porch. I don't intend becoming a human lightning rod."

"Be careful, dear," cautioned Mom.

"Hey, can I go too?" asked Mark.

"Sure," said Dad. "Put on your slippers first." It was just as Mr. Foster had thought. A huge limb lay out in the yard, narrowly missing their car.

"Wow!" said Mark. "That's a big one."

"Sure is. Well, let's get in the house." Both Sarah Jo and her mother were waiting at the bottom of the stairs."

"What did you see?" asked Sarah Jo.

"It was just as I suspected. A big limb down," answered her father. "More work to do. I'll have to get out the chain saw tomorrow."

"It's kind of creepy now. I don't want to go back to bed," said Sarah Jo.

"Why don't we all sit down here while the storm moves out of the area," said Mom. They all took places in the living room while the storm blustered and blew. The lights flickered, but stayed on.

"You know," said Dad. "This reminds me of a story I heard once when I was a boy. My grandfather told it to me after a big storm had gone through. That time a big elm had been struck by lightning, only the whole tree fell."

"Did anyone get hurt?" asked Mark.

"No, just the tree. It was a tall one."

"Wow!" said Sarah Jo.

"The thing is, no one ever thought that would happen because it was so strong and mighty."

"Then why did it?" asked Mark as he repositioned himself on the floor.

"Well, that's the funny thing about lightning, son. It usually strikes the highest object and at that time it was the tree. You've probably read about that in a book or online since you're into weather."

"I sure have, Dad," confirmed Mark. The storm soon abated and it was time to go back to bed. Thunder rumbled in the distance and a brief flash of lightning accompanied it several moments later.

"Sleep well, you two," said Mom. As Sarah Jo climbed into her bed she thought about that tall elm tree Dad had talked about. Maybe a person, like that tree, didn't need to be the biggest or the best to get noticed. She sure wouldn't want *that* kind of attention!

Chapter Five

The buzzing of Dad's chainsaw was too noisy to sleep through as Sarah Jo realized her father was following through on his plan to cut up last night's fallen limb. She and Callie and Abby planned to go to the mall, such as it was for a small town, to see what new clothes were in for school. Even though they wouldn't be attending public school it was a way to get caught up on their wardrobe and the clothes they'd need for fall and winter. Sarah Jo had saved up some money for them and Mom had helped out too. The girls planned to eat out as well which made it even more fun. Mom drove her over to Callie's and they'd walk to the mall from there. Abby was to meet them at Calico's, a store that featured reasonably priced clothing for families. As Sarah Jo and Callie were browsing through casual wear, Abby came bounding in.

"Hi guys!" Sarah Jo and Callie spun around in surprise.

"Nothing like a subtle entrance," giggled Callie.

"Hey Abby, what do you think of these?" Sarah Jo held up a pair of colorful pants that were elasticized at both waist and ankles with ballooning fabric between.

"What planet are *those* from?" asked Abby incredulously.

"No kidding!" added Callie. "Looks like they're part of a costume for a clown convention."

Sarah Jo held them up to her waist.

"What do you think people would say if I wore them to the Homecoming dance?" That brought giggles all around.

"Right," said Callie. "They'd be a hit for sure." After some serious shopping the girls decided they'd go to a cozy little restaurant known for its coffee, even though none of them really wanted any. The place was also known for their excellent soup and sandwiches which appealed to all of them.

"Good suggestion, Cal," said Abby. "Were you craving soup and a sandwich?"

"Well actually, I hope you don't mind, but Austin called me last night and asked me to lunch, but I said I already had plans for lunch. He asked if we'd mind if he stopped by here, which is why I suggested it for us."

"So Callie, what you're saying is that you and Austin already planned to meet here?" asked Sarah Jo.

"Yeh, pretty much. I figured you wouldn't mind. If you wanted to go somewhere else that would've been okay too."

"Uh Cal, the name of this place *is* Somewhere Else, remember?" asked Sarah Jo.

"Oh yeh, that's right." Callie laughed as she set her purchases on the floor next to her. The others followed suit.

"What does Austin want?" asked Abby.

"I'm not sure. Something about the dance, I think." The girls ordered and before long, three bowls of soup and three sandwiches arrived.

"I haven't had beef noodle soup in ages," said Callie as she dipped her spoon in, after they'd said a short grace.

"Same here for the tomato," remarked Abby. "How are your chicken and dumplings, Sarah Jo?"

"Yummy, of course!"

"Who, me?" asked Austin as he appeared as if from out of nowhere.

"You're silly!" said Callie. "Have a seat," she said as she motioned to the empty chair next to her.

"Don't mind if I do," obliged Austin. "What's cookin'?"

"Not much," said Abby after which she took a dainty bite of her sandwich.

"What's good here today?" he asked as he looked over the table of soup and sandwiches.

"Pretty much everything, I guess," said Callie.

"I'll go up and order something. Be right back." Sarah Jo noticed Austin had set his backpack next to his chair. He returned with a BLT and a glass of milk. "This oughta hold me for awhile."

"You wanted to talk to me, Austin?" asked Callie.

"Yeh, but it can wait till later. By the way, I want to thank you girls for letting me crash your get-togethers. It may seem that I don't have much of a life, but I do. I try and combine my stuff so I have time for everything." The girls finished up lunch and were planning to leave when Austin surprised them, "Let me catch this – lunch is on me."

"Well, thank you, Austin. That's very nice of you," said Sarah Jo.

"Yes it is," Callie chimed in.

"I'd say," added Abby.

"Hey ladies," said Austin. "I'm kind of doing an experiment and I could use your help, that is, if you want to."

"What's that?" asked Callie as she wiped her fingers with her napkin.

"Well, remember last time we were together – well except for you, Abby – and we played that game? It's that one called Spin and Win – or Not." Sarah Jo and Callie nodded. "Well, I'd like to see if I can outsmart it, for lack of a better way to put it."

"For what reason?" asked Sarah Jo.

"I spose to prove all things like it says in the Bible, but I also might write a paper on it – if I get some decent findings."

"So, what are you going to do to outsmart it?" asked Abby.

"I said *if* I can outsmart it," reminded Austin. He popped the last of his sandwich into his mouth.

"So, how do you accomplish that?" repeated Abby.

"I figure I can enlist you girls' help."

"In what way, Austin?" asked Callie.

"Well, let's come up with something here. The bunch of us should be able to come up with an idea or two with our combined brain power, you know." Austin got out the board with the spinner in the center. Who wants to go first?"

"I think you should," said Abby, as if daring him.

"Really? Well, okay." He gave the spinner the benefit of his muscular basketball arm.

"Wheeeee.." said Sarah Jo, teasing him. "Round and round we go -"

"Where it stops nobody knows," added Callie. They soon found out when the pointer aimed at the *y*. Sarah Jo spun next and the pointer pointed at the *o*. The following spin yielded a *u*. When the next letter came up *a*, they figured it was the beginning of the next word. Abby spun last and it was an *r*. Austin spun again and the pointer aimed at the *e*.

"This is crazy," declared Abby who'd been skeptical from the start.

"Crazy why?" said Callie. "It just says *you are*; so what? It's probably just coincidence."

"I wanna see where this is going," said Austin as he gave it another spin. It spun to the *i*. Another spin pointed to the *n*. After each of them taking a turn and Austin finishing out the remainder of spins, the result was *trouble84.*

"Now what could that mean? And who – *who* is in trouble?" asked Abby.

"I don't know, but I wanna find out," said Austin as he spun again, but every time he did the pointer aimed between letters or at a number.

"See?" said Abby. "It's just a silly piece of cardboard with a metal pointer in the middle. Why don't you throw it away and come up with a new experiment?"

"Well, if it actually spelled something, I'd sure like to know what the rest of it is," said Austin, more than a little annoyed.

"Hey, don't blow a gasket or else that silly piece of cardboard and metal already won," said Sarah Jo. "I've got to get going. If any of you figure it out, let me know." She stood up and gathered her bags.

"Don't you need a ride home or something?" asked Abby as she stood up.

"I'll call my mom."

"Hey, can I hitch a ride too?"

"Sure Abby. Not a problem. Bye Cal, bye Austin."

"Yeh, bye Callie and Austin," echoed Abby.

***

"Kinda crazy, that game of Austin's," said Abby as they waited for Mrs. Foster.

"Yeh, I like fun games, but this one's kind of off the wall. I wonder where he got it from. I haven't seen it in the stores or even online – not that I was looking for that kind of thing. I usually don't give games as gifts," said Sarah Jo. The girls found a bench to sit on while they waited.

"I wonder what Austin wanted to talk to Callie about."

"Who knows, Abby – especially when you're young and in love."

"In love! What do you know that you're not telling?"

"I'm kidding, Abby. I have no idea what they're talking about; probably has to do with the dance." As timing would have it, the Foster minivan pulled up.

"So did you girls have a good time?"

"We sure did, Mom," said Sarah Jo.

"We found some neat outfits, Mrs. Foster – all reasonably priced."

"Well then, your mother taught you well, Abby. No need to spend a fortune on clothes that will be out of fashion next year."

"I guess that's not the reason we bought them – cuz they'd be out of fashion eventually, but just cuz we liked them."

"I remember one year when I bought a couple pleated skirts, one with a sailor top," said Mom. Abby looked at Sarah Jo who shrugged. "A nice navy blue skirt and a white one. They cost me almost my whole clothing budget. I figured that the skirts and top would be interchangeable. I did wear them to school and even church, but by the next year they were out! No one would dare be caught wearing those styles."

"Wow..." said Abby. Mrs. Foster dropped off Abby and they continued back home.

"Well, are you looking forward to your last year of high school, dear?"

"Yes," replied Sarah Jo. "I really am." And she was.

Chapter Six

"Sarah Jo! You'll never guess what happened!" sputtered the voice over the phone.

"Chill, Callie! I can hardly understand you."

"It's Austin! Remember how he paid for our lunch yesterday?

"Yes, I do. That was very generous of -"

"Well, the police came by and paid him a call."

"What for, Callie?" Sarah Jo wondered what in the world they'd want with Austin.

"He passed a counterfeit twenty!" said the breathless Callie.

"What?" asked Sarah Jo incredulously.

"Yep, the twenty dollar bill he paid with wasn't real. He said he had to go down to the station and as the police put it, 'unravel' the mystery of where it came from."

"Poor Austin," said Sarah Jo.

"No kidding!"

"Well, where *did* it come from?"

"They haven't tracked it down to the source, but I guess that's what they're trying to do now."

"Where does that leave Austin? The poor guy doesn't need any more trouble in his life after what he's gone through over the past year."

"I don't know. I guess he can't be held accountable for something he didn't do."

"Callie! Maybe that's the '*trouble*' that crazy game spelled out."

"Oh my gosh! What if it is? How weird is *that*?"

"Well, it seems to be more than coincidence, doesn't it?" declared Sarah Jo. "Look, call me later if you find out anything, okay?"

"Hey, what's all the noise about?" asked Mark as he stuck his head in the doorway.

"Nothing that concerns you, Mr. Snoopy."

"Gosh, can't you be nice for a change? I was just asking."

"Yeh, well that's what snooping is – asking too many questions," said Sarah Jo as she shut her door. That's all she needed, having Mark inserting his nose into her business. Then if she caved and told him, he'd run and tell Mom and Dad. Even *she* didn't know what to think. She would tell Abby though. Abby would have a level-headed perspective on things she was sure. Abby didn't. In fact, she was quite upset. So once again she was on the phone, this time with Abby, trying to make sense out of things.

"Look Sarah Jo, I like Austin as much as anybody else but this is the second time this has happened. You told me about the sleepover. Now I'm kinda glad I wasn't there."

"It's not *his* fault, Abby. Do you think he sits at home cranking out funny money? I don't think so."

"Still, it's kinda weird. Maybe it's a leftover from that cult outfit he was in."

"I don't think so, Abby. Hey, I've got to get going. I have to fix dinner tonight and I don't have much of an appetite for anything." She decided on fried chicken since Mom had gone shopping yesterday after her volunteer work at the church. Baked potatoes and some green beans would complete the meal. Mom was particular about including the three food groups in a meal; like a meat, a carb like potatoes, and a vegetable. This dinner would be easy to do.

"Something sure smells good in here," said Mom as she entered the kitchen. "I appreciate your making dinner tonight. It gave me an opportunity to help out Mrs. Larkin with her canning. She sure is active for her age." Sarah Jo nodded.

"Can Mark set the table, Mom? He's just sitting at his computer probably doing something having to do with weather."

"He can – and will. I'll call him down here. Mark, come set the table!" Sarah Jo pondered that if she'd done the very same thing, it would be met with an argument. Parents sure have the power. I guess that's just the way God intended, she concluded as she topped the green beans with a couple pats of butter.

***

Sarah Jo didn't have to wait long to find out more about Austin. After dinner Callie called, this time with the rest of the story. Apparently, someone in Pine Moor was slipping these fake twenties into the system. The officer he'd spoken with said that they sometimes target smaller towns where vendors are more trusting, but he said only until it happens to *them* the first time. After that, there is no second time.

"Well,"said Callie; this sure seemed to fit the description of trouble to her way of thinking.

"Trouble is trouble is *trouble!*" she declared. "Just like that game said."

"Oh my gosh! Do you hear yourself? You're letting a game define an incident that could've happened anytime, anywhere."

"Sarah Jo! This is not a small thing. Do you realize it's a federal offense to pass bad money?"

"So, what did Austin say, I mean about what happened?"

"He just said that his conscience is clear and that he's never even been around anyone who's had this happen."

"Did you tell him about that goofy game?" asked Sarah Jo.

"Heck no! Why should I? He'll think I'm imagining stuff."

"Really, Callie? I mean *really?*"

"I think he figures that game is harmless – just cardboard and a metal pointer. That's all it is, right?"

"Seems like it to me, but I have to say Abby isn't too cool about it."

"What did you tell her, Sarah Jo?"

"Pretty much what you told me about things."

"And she said...?"

"Not much, Callie. I just think she kinda freaked out about it. I mean she wasn't there at the sleepover, so all she's hearing is what we've told her. If she saw that board and pointer she'd realize that it's all pretty innocent – more like coincidence."

"Yeh, why give so much power to something so stupid. Enough of that subject, let's talk about the dance. Are you excited?"

"I really am," said Sarah Jo. "Are you?"

"I guess so, well, if Austin leaves that goofy board game home that night." Sarah Jo chuckled.

"He's not going to bring it. I presume you're kidding."

"Uh, not really. With Austin you never know." Both girls laughed.

***

Fall seemed to come from out of nowhere and heralded its presence with cooler temperatures and falling leaves. Sarah Jo knew Homecoming was just around the corner and that meant the dance was too. She hoped the home team won, but she'd heard they weren't very good this year. There were quite a few rookies. Regardless of the outcome of the game, the dance would be fun, at least she hoped so. Luke Holman seemed like a nice guy but what could she tell from a voice on the phone? For that reason Sarah Jo called Callie and asked her if she and/ or Austin could set up something where they could all meet and where she could specifically meet Luke. It didn't make sense to her to meet at Homecoming and possibly feel uncomfortable with a perfect stranger. Callie agreed and they all decided to meet at Connie's the next afternoon, a Saturday, and the week before Homecoming.

The foursome crowded into a booth and ordered a favorite – Connie's cocoa. The weather was perfect for it.

"So Sarah Jo, how do you like home school? I mean is it tough?" asked Luke. She noticed his hands were rough and calloused, probably from work.

"No, actually it's quite easy. I get to pace myself and that helps."

"Pace yourself?" he questioned.

"Well, I mean I don't have a teacher demanding assignments by a certain time. But I do have to meet some deadlines. If I don't I'm only hurting myself."

"I guess that would kind of be like a football team without a coach," said Austin as he took a big gulp from the oversize cup. "I know our basketball team would be a mess without Coach Hardy."

"I'm not sure you can compare home school with sports," giggled Callie.

"Sure you can – and I just did," said Austin. They all laughed. They talked easily about various events at the school, as well as some of the teachers. It was hard for Sarah Jo to relate since she didn't know them. Still, it gave her a chance to see what her Homecoming escort would be like. She had to admit he never said one thing against any of the teachers or the school. That was a good sign.

"Hey Austin, you said something about a board game you've played with the girls. Don't you know board games are so yesterday – like about fifty years ago?"

"Luke, I was doing it for an experiment. There's a lot I missed out on when I was in my folks' church."

"Excuse me," interrupted Sarah Jo. "I don't mean to be rude but I'd hardly consider it to be a church." Austin took his last gulp of cocoa.

"You know what I mean, Sarah Jo; call it whatever you want," said Austin.

"Let's just say it's a knockoff of a real church," said Callie.

"You're being way too generous, Cal," said Sarah Jo. "I think it's exactly what it wants to be; sort of a cult in church's clothing, you know, like a wolf in sheep's clothing?"

"Well anyway, I'd still like to prove my point with Spin and Win – or Not! How about one last time with it?"

"When, Austin, on the night of the dance?" asked Sarah Jo.

"No, how about right now?"

"Don't tell me you brought it along," said Sarah Jo.

"I did," declared Austin. "It's right here in my backpack." One never knew since Austin brought his backpack with him almost everywhere.

"What do you say? Should we give it a try and put these issues to rest once and for all?" Sarah Jo grimaced.

"I spose," said Callie reluctantly. "Boy, if Abby was here she'd go nuts."

"Why?" asked Austin. "She knows how it works."

"That's the whole point," said Sarah Jo. Luke just looked perplexed and said nothing. Once again the board and spinner came out and each took a turn spinning. The first two spins were gibberish, just babble. The words Sarah Jo and Callie seemed to spell out were: *dontb5shookedif8.*

"What kind of a message is that?" asked Luke.

"Spin, Luke and maybe we'll find out," said Austin. Luke spun the spinner with the tip of his finger and sent it flying madly. "Hey, you don't have to wreck it though."

"Uh, sorry." One by one the letters spelled out a strange word then ended with a number.

"I think you're done," said Austin, noting that the word seemed to finish with a number.

"Let's see," said Callie. "Luke spun the word *dangger3?* What's that sposed to mean?"

"I have to take my turn, then maybe we'll find out." Austin spun and each time a letter appeared and Callie wrote them down just as she had the others.

"It says *seeeksyu8,*" said Callie. "That doesn't make any sense."

"Wait a minute," said Austin. "Let's try and figure this out."

"Well, if that spells something, I think Mr. Spinner needs to go back to school," said Sarah Jo. "I mean if that actually says something, it would be a shocker."

"Hey, that's it!" said Austin, his eyes lighting up. "That word in the first part that Callie and Sarah Jo spun might say 'shocked'."

"Only it doesn't," said Luke. "It says *shooked.* What is that sposed to mean?"

"No, I think that means shocked," said Austin. "I mean it has to make sense." Callie and Sarah Jo looked at one another, perplexed.

"Wait! I think it says: 'don't be shocked if danger seeks you', said Luke. "Who is it referring to?"

"Hold on a sec. You act like it's actually telling us something. It's just a game," said an annoyed Sarah Jo.

"Well, it would help to know who or what it's referring to," said Austin. "I mean don't you want to know?"

"Not especially. I mean why would I go to cardboard and metal to find something out?" asked Sarah Jo as she gathered her clutch and jacket.

"Hey wait, SJ. It's a game meant for fun. Let's follow through on this," said Austin.

"You three can do that on your own. I'd rather forget about it and get on to something important."

"Let me walk you out, Sarah Jo," said Luke. He got up and followed Sarah Jo to the door.

"Leaving so soon?" asked Connie from behind the counter. "Free refills on the cocoa today."

"Thanks Connie, but I've got to get home. The other three might like more though." Once outside, Luke brought to mind the reason they all met there to begin with.

"It was nice meeting you, Sarah Jo. I look forward to the dance – and, of course, the game."

"Me too. Hoping for a victory. Bye now."

"See you this weekend," said Luke.

Chapter Seven

Sarah Jo had to admit she was excited about the dance. It definitely helped that the home team won, albeit a squeaker. It didn't matter though. The main thing was that they had won and everyone was in high spirits for the upcoming dance. The guys would stop by Callie's and pick her up first, then Sarah Jo. She'd be ready! She took one final look in the mirror and figured she would be more than passable. She had to remind herself that it wasn't the outside appearance that makes a person, but who a person is from within. She put on the sterling pendant with the turquoise stone that she'd gotten for her birthday. All but forgotten was the "message" provided by Austin's game/experiment from earlier in the week. They'd concluded that it was just a hodge-podge of words randomly that came together. The fact that there were actually words was merely coincidence, but the unsuspecting dabblers were in for a rude awakening.

Sarah Jo's father opened the door upon hearing a couple of knocks and he invited Luke in. As if on cue, her mother went to get Sarah Jo from her room.

"Honey, your date is here," she announced. "He looks like such a nice young man."

"Told ya, Mom."

"Have you got everything, dear?"

"Mom," said a quasi-annoyed Sarah Jo. "I'm not moving out."

"Of course not," laughed Mrs. Foster. "But you might want to take a tissue or two. Years ago we'd bring a hankie with us."

"Hankie?"

"A handkerchief, you know, just in case."

"Mom, this is going to be fun, not a tear fest." Sarah Jo noted the quizzical look on her mother's face. "You know, it's sposed to be fun, not a drag."

"Sarah Jo, where are you picking up these terms from?"

"Mom, I think you had a few of those in your day, as you'd put it."

"True honey, but each generation is supposed to be an improvement over the last."

"You're so funny, Mom. Now where is my scarf?" She found her light jacket and the matching scarf nd slid by Mom. Luke stood near the door as if he was ready to bolt. Even so, he looked sharp. His eyes lit up when he saw Sarah Jo.

"You look great," he observed.

"Thanks, so do you," answered Sarah Jo. Mr. Foster cleared his throat.

"Have her home by midnight. The dance is over at eleven and the extra hour will give you time to get something to eat and drive home."

"Daaad," whined Sarah Jo painfully.

"Yes sir, not a problem," replied Luke as he opened the door.

"Have a good time," Mrs. Foster called out after them.

***

"Hi Callie, hi Austin," greeted Sarah Jo as she slid into the front seat. Luke got in on his side and reminded everyone to buckle up.

"You sound like my mom," said Callie.

"Hopefully more like your dad, a few octaves lower."

"Well yeh, but you know what I meant."

"Yes I did. Okay, everyone ready for some fun?" Fun sounded good to Sarah Jo and they soon seemed to be in the right place for it. The gym was decked out in fall attire with its orange and brown streamers as well as pumpkins and corn stalks. Team colors and mascot were also a part of the décor. Familiar songs blared from the speakers and the dance floor was packed. Time flew and the dance was over, much to everyone's regret. Sarah Jo was breathless from all the excitement. She could see why society and its traditions were so appealing – those traditions, even without God as the focal point – were fun!

"Okay," said Luke, "I guess we have just enough time to grab a snack somewhere, then I have to get this lady home."

"Yes, my dad is really into being punctual," said Sarah Jo. Once again they got into Luke's sensible sedan.

"This car is going to have to go once I head off to college," Luke declared. "I'll get one that's got more pizazz."

"When you're in college you won't be able to afford to get the flashy car, Luke," said Austin. "I think it's kind of humbling to ride a bike, but I'm saving up for college."

"Well, you've got a point there," admitted Luke. "This thing costs plenty for gas and maintenance – plus insurance, even if I am on my family's policy. Teen drivers have high rates and I have to help out with the premiums." They pulled out of the lot and decided to go to Burger Station, a new fast food place on the edge of town. The couples had just gotten inside the empty restaurant and settled into a booth when soon after a gaunt young man in a dark blue hoodie came over and stood next to where Sarah Jo was sitting.

"Give me your money and no one gets hurt. I have a gun in my pocket." Sarah Jo felt that gun poke into her side. She detected a spirit of desperation in the guy's voice and said a prayer immediately. These kinds of things happened all the time, but never here in Pine Moor. Austin, who was sitting on the outside across from Sarah Jo, started to get to his feet.

"No," said Sarah Jo. "Let's just give him our money." She dug into her clutch purse and pulled out a ten dollar bill. She was glad she hadn't brought more. The others followed suit.

"Now, go take this to the counter and get me two mega burgers and large fries," he ordered Austin as he handed him Sarah Jo's ten. "And don't say nothing else to the chick at the counter. My gun will be right where it is till you come back. I'm sure you don't want to be responsible for having someone get hurt." Austin got up and followed through. When he returned he gave the order and the change to the thief.

"Want me to count out the change for you?" asked Austin.

"Shut up!" hissed the young captor. "Now give me your cell phones." The smell of the hamburgers and fries made Sarah Jo nauseous. They produced the phones, except for Sarah Jo. "Where's yours?"

"It wouldn't fit into my clutch purse," she explained. "It's at home."

"Now listen," he warned in a bare whisper. "You sit here like nothing's wrong. Don't move till I'm outa here." They obeyed his orders then got out of the booth. Austin ran to the counter and told the girl to call the police.

"We've been robbed," he said. "At gunpoint!" Luke checked to make sure Sarah Jo was okay.

"I-I guess so." She wasn't hurt physically, but she was shaken up by the robbery.

"I should've let you sit on the inside, but you headed off to the restroom so I just slid in and stayed there." Two police officers arrived on the scene and one asked for details which all four provided. The other officer questioned the girl at the counter, as well as the cook.

"He also took our cell phones, officer," said Callie.

"That's helpful information. We may be able to locate him with that alone. I'll need your phone numbers." By the time the officers had left, Sarah Jo noticed the time. It was long after eleven o'clock. She asked to use the store's phone so she could call her parents. Her mother answered and was in a near panic when she heard what Sarah Jo had to say. She put Sarah Jo's father on and he peppered her with questions. He would be right down there, even though Sarah Jo assured him that there was no need and that they were heading home.

"Stay there!" commanded Mr. Foster. "You don't know where that crazy might be." It turned out they had no choice. The thief had the presence of mind to slash the front tire of Luke's car. As the rest waited, Luke changed the tire and just finished up as Sarah Jo's father pulled into the lot. Luke explained that he would've had Sarah Jo home on time had it not been for the thief.

"I know that, son. I can tell you're a responsible young man. Too bad that kid wasn't more like you. The way you get money is by working for it, not robbing people."

"Yes sir," replied Luke. It was an evening that Sarah Jo, and for that matter all of them, would never forget. Sarah Jo realized her life could've been over in a split second. On the way home Dad praised her for her quick thinking of telling the others to just give him their money.

"That alone could have saved your life, honey. Well, not *just* that. You were doing your part. But it perhaps was the Holy Spirit putting that thought into your head and you acting on it. I can see God's hand in all of this." Sarah Jo noticed that Mom was visibly relieved at seeing her.

"My goodness, dear, you've had quite a night!"

"Yes, and I'm tired. I think I'll go to bed, if you don't mind."

"That's fine, dear. If you feel like talking about it in the morning, I'll be here for you."

"Thanks, Mom." As she lay in bed, Sarah Jo recalled the image of this guy and how creepy he looked – and acted. She prayed that she wouldn't have a nightmare about him and that whoever he was, the police would catch him soon.

***

Although the morning sun shone bright it didn't seem that life would ever be quite the same again. Sarah Jo was glad it was Sunday and that she could escape to the security of church. Ironically, the sermon had to do with the wiles of the devil, a subject Pastor didn't preach on very often. Although she didn't hang on his every word, Sarah Jo had to admit she was interested. This was especially true when he used John 10:10 to make his point. She listened as he read the scripture:

"'The thief does not come except to steal, and to kill, and to destroy. I have come that they may have life, and that they may have it more abundantly.'" He cleared his throat. "That, my friends, tells us a lot about life." Suddenly, those words resonated with Sarah Jo. She knew who the Thief was, and how he manifests himself. She remembered the verse that said, "by their fruits you shall know them". This was how to identify good and evil – or at least *one* way. Was the thief – *their* thief – just hungry, looking for a burger or two to eat? No, he could've just come up and asked if someone could spare a buck or two. Maybe it was for drugs or even cigarettes. No one would knowingly provide someone with that kind of money for those purposes.

"And so, brethren, in conclusion, we see here that although our enemy has power, it pales in comparison to that of the Holy Spirit which we have access to. We need never be afraid, for it's the devil who is afraid of that awesome mighty power of God. Please take your hymnals and rise." As her family left, Sarah Jo sought out Callie.

"So, how are you doing after last night?" she asked her.

"Way to wreck a homecoming dance date, huh?"

"Right? Wonder if they'll find the creep," said Sarah Jo doubtfully.

"Hey, we've got a small department here, but our cops are top notch."

"That is true." Sarah Jo had forgotten that Callie's uncle was on the Pine Moor Police Department, or PMPD, as Callie referred to it.

"Hey, I heard you two had quite a night last night."

"Abby! I was going to call you and tell you about it. I went to bed pretty much as soon as I got home last night."

"It's okay. I saw it on the news this morning, not that I usually watch the morning news, but Dad does."

"Did they mention names?" asked Abby.

"No, but they showed some footage from a camera in the place. I knew it was you guys cuz I saw Sarah Jo's outfit – or part of it anyway. Besides, I figured that was Austin cuz he's so tall. It showed him walking to the counter. I didn't see the face but I figured it was him. Bet you two were scared, huh?"

"I don't know; it was all so surreal. Like in slow motion," volunteered Sarah Jo.

"Well, you kept your wits about you, as they say."

"Maybe it seemed that way, but I was praying the whole time.

Something – maybe the Holy Spirit – told me to just give him what he wanted which was money."

"Well, that was the smart thing to do," said Abby. "They say if you're ever involved in a stickup to just give the robber what he asks for. It sure is better than losing your life." Later that day, Sarah Jo mulled over the events of the night before. The dance had been fun and Callie and Austin seemed to have fun too. As far as dates were concerned – and she really wasn't too concerned about dating – they made a great foursome in terms of double dating. One thing bothered her though. She liked Austin well enough and he had fit into the church and its activities but he somehow seemed, well, different. But different from *what?* That thought puzzled her right up until bedtime and even as she drifted off to sleep.

Chapter Eight

School was fun! Maybe it was because of her diligence during past years of study, but she felt this one was going to be a breeze. At the end of the school day she was going to meet up with Abby since she'd kind of neglected her of late. They decided to meet at Corky's, an old standby in Pine Moor. It used to be a root beer stand where carhops – Mom had told her about them – used to skate up to customers' cars to take and deliver orders. Sarah Jo couldn't imagine the old fashioned skates and not roller blades. But now the establishment was simply a coffee house, with other items on the menu too. It wasn't like Connie's where she felt like she was going to a Swiss Chalet, but rather a no-frills cafe. No way would she ever go back to that Burger Station where she could have lost her life. That memory was scorched into her mind.

The day slipped by quickly and she found herself sitting at a corner table awaiting Abby's arrival. For a split second she thought she might see Austin burst through the door since he had crashed a couple other meet-ups with her friends. Well, she reasoned, it was probably because of Callie. He did seem to have feelings for his rescuer. A more mature outlook would be to realize it wasn't Callie who had done the rescuing, but God. Callie was just the instrument. She gazed into the cup of cocoa on the table before her. It was almost as good as Connie's.

"Hey, Sarah Jo. *You're* deep in thought."

"Oh hi, Abby. Well, not really *deep* in thought, just thinking."

"Well, my mom always used to say to me 'a penny for your thoughts' but it looks like yours are worth a lot more than a penny."

"Not when it's just about cocoa," laughed Sarah Jo.

"So – what's up?"

"The sky," offered Sarah Jo. She took a sip of her cocoa.

"Oh come on, that's an old one. Hang on while I go get some cocoa." Abby returned almost as quickly as she left. Her bright red mug was steaming with the cocoa topped with mini marshmallows. "You're not getting anything to eat?"

"No, this cocoa is filling," said Sarah Jo, taking another sip.

"So, exactly what happened over there at that burger place, Sarah Jo? I mean you were really looking forward to the dance." Sarah Jo gave a blow-by-blow account of the evening but it made her uncomfortable to recall it. "So, that's about it, Abby."

"Wow – mega wow!"

"I know!"

"You never know when something bad is going to happen, right?"

"That's for sure, Abby."

"So, have you talked to the others about it?"

"Not yet, but they want to get together and talk about it. They figured it might be helpful. Hey, you're welcome to join us if you want to."

"Uh, no thanks, SJ, I'll pass. I get chills just thinking about what *you* told me now." Abby checked her phone. It seemed to hold her attention.

"Hey Abby, I didn't come here to watch you with your phone."

"Don't you have yours along? I mean it won't insult *me* if you check it."

"Sure, I have it with me. Remember, mine didn't fit in my clutch purse for the dance so I left it at home. That's why I still have it, unlike the others. But Mom told me it's really rude to use my phone when I'm with others unless it's an emergency, so I followed her advice."

"Oh, sorry," apologized Abby. "Didn't mean to ignore you."

"Well, it must've been pretty important to interrupt us."

"Not really. It was just a text to pick up some cinnamon from the store. I guess Mom's going to be making an apple crisp or something."

"Yeh, my mother does that to me too sometimes. I guess these phones really can be helpful. I just can't imagine the days before we had them," said Sarah Jo.

"Right? So, you're going to meet Callie, Austin and Luke, huh?"

"Something like that. It was a thought anyway."

"Go for it, SJ! You have a lot of good ideas." The girls talked about school and the Heaven Club at church for a while. "Well, I'd better get that cinnamon and head home. Mom will need it pretty soon."

"Okay. Glad we got a chance to meet up for some girl talk and stuff," said Sarah Jo.

"I spose the 'and stuff' was the cocoa?" Abby giggled.

"Whatever, Abby," laughed Sarah Jo. It was kind of funny. They hadn't really talked about anything of substance, but that was what made it fun to get together with Abby. On the way home she decided to call Callie and set up something. The day was brisk but the sun shone warm, and the leaves were beginning to change color and drop to the ground. It was a good day to be out.

"Hi Callie, it's Sarah Jo."

"I know. Our phone has caller ID," came the voice at the other end.

"When are you going to get another phone, I mean one just for you?" asked Sarah Jo.

"I'm not sure. Mom said that their plan would provide a replacement, but so far, nothing. So she got me one of those kind you load minutes on, just so I'll have something for an emergency, as she put it."

"Oh, okay. Well, I guess it'll work if you need *something*. Hey, I was just thinking it might be sort of a good idea if you and Austin and Luke and I got together."

"For what?"

"Well, I just thought maybe to talk since we all went through the same thing that night, Cal." She stepped off the curb and checked for traffic, then resumed her walk home. He heart skipped a beat when she saw a teenager in a gray hoodie coming her way. Of course it wasn't *him,* she reassured herself, but it brought back the raw memories.

"Sarah Jo, are you there? Sarah Jo?"

"Huh.. oh, sorry. I thought I saw that creep, but it was just a kid with a football. I'm sure that thief wouldn't be out where he could be seen."

"You mean hiding in plain sight?" asked Callie.

"Thanks a lot. That really helps, Callie." The boy, who looked nothing like the criminal, passed her with out incident. He was wrapped up in the music he was listening to through his earbuds. "Well anyway, do you think you guys would like to maybe come over to my place sometime soon just to talk about what we went through? It might help, you know."

"I don't know, Sarah Jo. Guys aren't very good at that."

"Why not? It's sort of like those shows where they talk to the victims afterward. It can really help people face their fears."

"Yeh, like guys are going to admit they were afraid. How does *that* happen?"

"You act like they're from another planet," said Sarah with a giggle.

"Well, aren't they?"

"Callie, you're funny."

"Look, I'll check with the guys if you want. When would be a good time to get together?"

"How about Saturday afternoon, maybe about two o'clock? I'll have some snacks and make sure that Mark's not going to pester us. Does that sound like it will work?"

"Sure, why not? I'll let you know what the guys say about it."

"Well, I don't think they'll turn down snacks. Tell them I'm making a great nacho dip," chuckled Sarah Jo. "I don't think they'll pass nachos up."

***

Later, Sarah Jo noticed that Callie had sent her an email. Upon opening it she read: *hey, I checked with Austin and he texted Luke.. everything's set for Saturday at two.. see you then.*

Okay, so it was all set. She ran it by Mom and Dad at dinner and they okayed it. If it was nice out they could gather on the deck; if not, they could use the family room downstairs. That room didn't get a lot of use but Dad said a finished basement was always a plus – as long as it didn't leak.

***

That Saturday, at two o'clock promptly, there was a knock at the door. Since it was chilly out, Callie and Austin had ridden over with Luke. They had also brought cider, much to Sarah Jo's appreciation. The warmth of the house mingled with the fragrance of pizza which Sarah Jo had popped into the oven and, true to her word, she had whipped up some nacho dip as well.

"Hey guys, just put your coats up on the rack. Then you can help bring the snacks and stuff downstairs."

"Wow! You went all out, didn't you, Sarah Jo?" noticed Callie.

"I guess so. It's cold out so I figured that would probably call for a little more sustenance."

"Sustenance?" questioned Austin. "Oh, you mean food."

"Right," replied Sarah Jo. They all brought something downstairs and settled into the casual sofa and chairs arranged in front of a fireplace.

"Do you ever use that?" asked Luke nodding toward the fireplace.

"Sometimes, but usually not so early in the fall. We mostly use it for special occasions when it gets colder." They all served themselves the food they'd brought down.

"Mmmm, this is good, Sarah Jo," said Callie, referring to the nacho dip.

"Hey, the pizza's not bad either," said Austin, as he took a generous bite from the slice he held.

"Okay, now that we've taken care of creature comforts here, let's get into the reason I suggested we meet," said Sarah Jo.

"Then why don't you start?" asked Callie.

"Well okay. It's not like a fun time we all had though. It's kind of hard to talk about, but it's still clear in my mind."

"I don't think any of us will forget it," added Luke.

"You got that right!" said Austin emphatically.

"I think the bad part was that it caught us all off guard," said Sarah Jo. "I mean we were all on a high from Pine Moor winning and wanted to finish off the night with something to eat. Who would've thought it almost ended in tragedy?" Callie visibly shivered.

"That's creepy, Sarah Jo. Are you sure you aren't exaggerating?"

"You're not the one who had a gun poked in your side." She took a small bite of pizza and set the piece down. "What about you guys? How are you doing after all this?" Luke glanced over to Austin.

"It caught me off guard for sure," said Luke.

"Yeh, me too," agreed Austin.

"On the positive side, it got me a new set of tires. My dad's insurance covered it," said Luke. Sarah Jo rolled her eyes.

"What's with you guys? It that your takeaway from that terrible situation? New tires?"

"Hey, those things are expensive. You ought to go price them sometime on your computer," said Luke.

"Well, that's the *only* positive that I can see," said Sarah Jo. "Wait, I take that back. I've learned something - I will never eat at that burger place again."

"You didn't eat there the first time," said Callie. "None of us got the chance."

"And I never want to," said Sarah Jo.

"So, is this the reason we came here – to be restaurant critics?" asked Austin. He took another slice of pizza. "Now *this* is good eating right here."

"Of course not," replied Sarah Jo. "Right now none of us is really opening up."

"This might help," suggested Austin as he pulled out the now familiar board game, Spin and Win – or Not! The girls groaned.

"Whaaat.." questioned Austin impatiently. "It's just a game, but it might lighten things up a little here."

"Don't look at *me*, man," said Luke. "I don't know the history here with that thing." Austin made room on the table for the board. Before long each had taken their turn resulting in a hodge podge of letters.

"Your genie must be taking a nap," said Callie.

"Genie?" echoed Sarah Jo.

"I'm just saying those letters make no sense.

"Okay, now try it," urged Austin, glancing at Luke.

"Who – *me?*"

"Yes, who do you think I meant?"

"Hey, relax, Austin. It's just a game." After another couple of rounds of letters and numbers between, the result was: *too4late7now*

"Let's keep going. That alone doesn't make sense at all," said Callie. When they had finished it read: *all2in8peril*

"All in peril?" asked Sarah Jo. "That's crazy talk."

"Weird message..." Callie's voice trailed off.

"Hey, come on," said Luke. "This is just a goofy board game. As my dad would say, 'I don't set such store by something like this'."

"Of course not!" declared Austin as he folded the board and put it and the spinner back into his backpack.

"Hey, I've been accused of being sensible," laughed Sarah Jo, "and this thing doesn't make any sense to me at all. She reached for her half eaten slice of pizza. At that precise moment, the sound of footsteps on the basement stairs followed by the startling sound of someone tumbling down to the bottom moaning in pain, brought everyone to their feet and to the source.

"Mark! Is that you?" called Mom from the kitchen. Mark lay on the basement floor, stunned by his fall.

"Mark, are you okay?" asked an agitated Sarah Jo as she knelt over him.

"Hey bud," said Luke, "do we need to call the paramedics?" Mom rushed down the stairs to find her son crumpled in a heap at the bottom of the stairs.

"Mark! Sarah Jo, go get your dad from the yard!" Sarah Jo obeyed without hesitation. What had happened? Why was Mark on the steps anyway? Was he eavesdropping? Mom had told him to leave us alone.

"Dad, come quick! There's been an accident!" Her father ran across the yard from where he'd been raking.

"What's wrong?" he asked. Worry lines creased his forehead.

"Mark fell down the basement stairs. I think he's hurt." Sarah Jo followed her father as he dashed across the yard and into the house.

"What happened here?" demanded Dad.

"I-I missed a step, I think," said Mark choking back tears in an attempt to be brave.

"You sure did," said Dad. "You missed *something* for sure. Peg, I think we should call the paramedics. If he's broken something we don't want to make it worse by moving him."

"No Dad," said Mark. "I can get up." He moved his legs and made an effort to get to his feet. "I'm okay."

"Are you sure, son? I think we'd better take you in anyway. One of you boys here give me a hand in helping Mark to the car." Luke jumped to his feet to help. "I'll call you, Peg, as soon as I find out something."

"Okay dear," said Mom with a note of trepidation in her voice.

"It'll be okay, Mom," said Sarah Jo. "It just looks like Mark got shook up a bit. At least the floor is carpeted. I wonder what he was doing at the top of the stairs. I thought he was going to leave us alone."

"He probably smelled the pizza," said Callie, trying to inject some humor into the situation.

"Probably so," said Mom weakly. Anything humorous about the situation appeared to be lost on her.

"Back," said Luke as he descended the stairs. "Mr. Foster said he didn't need help at the ER. So, here I am."

"I don't know if we should continue here," said Sarah Jo. "What do you think, guys?"

"There's nothing we can do for Mark at the moment," said Callie. "Well, except to pray."

"Good idea," said Mom. "Mind if I join you?" Sarah Jo asked Austin to lead in prayer and he did, though reluctantly. Sarah Jo breathed a sigh of relief when the last amen was said.

***

As it turned out, Mark had not broken anything, according to Sarah Jo's mother who informed the group downstairs. They all agreed it was time to break up. Not much had been accomplished by gathering, but the four left things open-ended for a future discussion.

"I'm glad your brother's going to be okay, Sarah Jo," said Luke. "He sure put on a brave face."

"Yeh, he may be little but he's tough," said Sarah Jo as the trio walked out the front door to Luke's car. "See you guys."

"Did you accomplish anything down there?" asked Mom who was bustling around the kitchen preparing dinner and tending to Mark who was in the recliner in the living room. "Here. Take this to your brother for his leg." She handed Sarah Jo an ice pack.

"To answer your question Mom, no, because nobody wanted to talk. I think they were almost at the point of saying something, but then Mark had his accident."

"Oh, that's too bad. You were hoping they'd open up."

"Mom, Mark shouldn't have been snooping anyway. If he hadn't he wouldn't have fallen."

"That may be so, Sarah Jo, but I'm not going to bring it up to him now, nor should you."

***

It was only until that night when Sarah Jo was talking to Abby that a thought occurred to her. Abby, as usual, had lots of questions.

"You say you didn't get into the details of what happened on Homecoming night at that restaurant?"

"I was willing, Abby, but no one else had much to say about it."

"That's weird. You'd think they'd have plenty to say."

"Well, we were eating pizza. Kind of hard to talk when you're eating, you know."

"And that was all – just eating pizza?"

"No, not exactly all. We were playing that game that Austin has -"

"*What?*" Why do I keep hearing about that stupid game?"

"Austin says he's doing an experiment with it."

"What *kind* of experiment?" asked Abby impatiently.

"I don't know. I guess just to see if predictions that it makes actually happen."

"*What?*" That's crazy! What are cardboard and a metal pointer going to predict?"

"I don't know, Abby. All I know is he brings that game with him every time we get together. Maybe he even takes it everywhere he goes."

"So, did you keep on using it?"

"Not exactly. I heard a noise at the top of the basement stairs and the next thing we knew, Mark was laying at the bottom."

"Oh. My. Gosh. It seems like every time you guys get together and you use that thing, something freaky happens."

"Abby, now don't turn drama queen on me."

"I should hang up on you, Sarah Jo. I was just making an observation, which is also what goes on in an experiment. Let's just say this is *my* contribution." Sarah Jo had to admit that Abby did make sense. What was the connection between Austin and that stupid game of his? Could it be just coincidence that every time they played it, weird stuff would happen?

Chapter Nine

As the school year progressed, Sarah Jo decided she would try to accomplish two things: get very serious about her courses and make the most of each one, and try to enjoy social opportunities that came her way. Of course, the spiritual aspect trumped all so she applied herself in that way too. She still had nightmares about that Homecoming weekend and what happened at that restaurant. Still, she wasn't going to let the devil steal her peace. She knew God was much stronger than some nasty lowlife. Well, she had to admit that in some cases a person like him had unfortunate circumstances like being born into a family who didn't know God or had fallen prey to temptation. But, she also reasoned, with a church on nearly every street corner – well, maybe not *every* – it was hard to believe that someone like him had not heard about God or redemption. Plus there were numerous televangelists who usually ended their shows with the gospel message and an altar call. Just no excuse not to know about Jesus.

Thanksgiving was less than a month away. Halloween had come and gone, but Sarah Jo wasn't convinced that it had children's best interest at heart. She herself actually went trick or treating once when she was about seven, and that time with Dad who said she should experience it at least once. When they got back home, Dad told her to dump her candy out on the kitchen table. To her, it seemed like treasure but Dad and Mom explained the bad part about eating too much candy.

"Sarah Jo, how do you like going to the dentist and having a cavity drilled and then filled?" Sarah Jo remembered wincing at the time and saying she didn't like it at all. So then Mom said she could pick out a candy bar to eat right away and then go brush her teeth so it couldn't cause a cavity. She got to do that night after night until her candy supply was gone. Of course, she offered a bar of their choosing to Mom and Dad on that first night.

She had to admit that she loved Christmas! Of course, she always liked new things but she also liked the giving part. It was fun to imagine what her parents and her brother would like and then go shopping for those things. Sometimes she actually had to go out shopping to come up with ideas for them, but the fun part was to imagine how they'd react on Christmas morning when they opened their gifts. Sarah Jo felt bad for families who didn't have it as good as hers did. She couldn't even imagine what it was like to not have gifts to open, but some kids didn't or maybe only got one and no more. For that reason she saved out enough money to purchase a present for a child whose name ended up being on a paper ornament on the Giving Tree at SmartMart.

Buying a gift for Mark this year would be easy – anything basketball. He'd been accepted on the home school team and had practiced regularly for weeks now. He had confessed that the reason he had fallen down the basement stairs was simply because he'd hoped he could talk to Austin about basketball, and maybe grab a quick slice of pizza as well. Sarah Jo admonished him, saying that it didn't make it right and that he should have waited until the group came upstairs.

Gifts for Mom and Dad would be a different story. She might get a joint gift but couldn't imagine what it might be – maybe something for the house? She still had time. After all, Thanksgiving itself was a couple weeks away. So she had plenty of time.

What bothered her was the fact that the thief that had terrorized her and the group at the Burger Station after the Homecoming dance had not been found. Dad had inquired more than once but the police chief could only say that the department was still working on it. Callie's and Austin's and Luke's phones hadn't been used and, of course, Sarah Jo's had been left at home. The chief promised he would contact Dad the moment they caught up with the man. He had cautioned Sarah Jo and the rest of the group, to observe safe practices such as not going out alone at night which, he emphasized, was just good common sense. The message was lost on her because she couldn't think of anything she'd rather *not* do.

***

"Is that you, dear?" asked Mom when Sarah Jo entered the kitchen after raking the yard.

"Yes, and I've never seen so many leaves. You know, at first they're kind of pretty like in late September when a couple float down from the trees, but they're not so pretty when they come down in bushel baskets full and they're brown and crispy. Mark can finish up the yard. I did most of it."

"He's been practicing down at the park every day now I think, but I'll make sure he takes his turn at it. I'll just tell him it'll strengthen his arms for basketball which I'm sure it does."

"I am proof of that," confirmed Sarah Jo as she flexed her arms. After dinner, Sarah Jo got a call from Callie. She closed the door to her room, mainly because Mark was known to snoop in from the hallway on her conversations. It didn't make sense to her since a person couldn't get much from a one-sided conversation.

"So what's going on?" asked Sarah Jo as she flopped down on her bed.

"Well, I talked to Austin for one thing."

"And..?"

"Ummm... I don't know if you're going to like this or not but Austin said that Luke would like to go out with you again, this time on a normal date."

"Normal as in not being held up at a restaurant, you mean?"

"Exactly!" confirmed Callie.

"What else did Austin say?"

"The guys are wondering if the four of us can go out again, this time *without* the thief.

"That's a funny way to put it; I mean it really is sort of funny," chuckled Sarah Jo.

"I agree."

"Yeh, it could be kind of therapeutic when you think about it."

"Thera – what?"

"It has to do with treatment of a condition; in our case a bad experience." Sarah Jo rearranged her hair on her pillow.

"Cool. By the way, I asked Austin about that game and its messages."

Sarah Jo groaned inwardly. "Do I want to know what he said?"

"He said he is almost done with his experiment," replied Callie. "Just one or two more experiences should do it, he told me."

"So far, I haven't heard one positive thing from that board – not one!"

"Relax, Sarah Jo. It's not like he worships that game."

"He might as well, He takes it everywhere with him. I wonder if he takes it to school with him."

"Nah – I don't think he's *that* dedicated to it," said Callie, dismissing the notion.

"Well, if we double date again, he can leave that fifth wheel at home. Hey, that's kinda funny cuz that game has a wheel."

"Sarah Jo, you should do stand-up," giggled Callie. "We could all use a good laugh now and then."

"Hey, I gotta go. Mom's calling me. Talk to you later. Bye Cal."

Later, as Sarah Jo lay in her bed waiting to drift off, she pondered her conversation with Callie. What *was* the connection Austin had to that board game? Why did he seem to have it with him wherever he went? There were lots of board games that people played. Maybe they weren't as popular now as years ago since kids liked playing video games; so did some adults. Sarah Jo heard the lonesome moan of a freight train in the distance as it wended its way through Pine Moor. She shivered even though she wasn't cold. Should she push Callie to find out more about the game or was she just making too much of it all? She never saw Austin with it when he was still in Future Life Fellowship. For that matter, Fern Samuels never made any reference to such a game either. Being such a "pillar in the church" she would surely know such a thing. But Sarah Jo didn't plan to ask her – or Austin for that matter.

***

The next day it rained and the one after that too. It was the kind of rain that heralds the settling in of fall, a warning that winter is on its way. Cold raindrops driven by the northwest wind splatted on what was left of the leaves on the trees as well as those on the ground. The drops made large circle stains on the sidewalks. No one in their right mind would want to go out on such a day unless they absolutely had to.

"But Sarah Jo," argued Abby, "I need to see you today."

"Why does it have to be today, Abby? Why not tomorrow?"

"It just can't. It needs to be today. I need for you to meet me at Somewhere Else. Remember that place where they have great soups and sandwiches?"

"Yes, I know the place, but I'm not going out in this rain. By the way, has it occurred to you that this is a school day?"

"Of course, Sarah Jo, but people *do* go out for lunch. I'm not worried about it. Mom has some shopping to do so I asked if she could pick you up. She said yes."

"What time?" asked Sarah Jo.

"How about eleven?"

"Wow! That's a half hour from now. Okay, well I'll be ready."

"Great. See you then." Sarah Jo remembered that she wanted to take advantage of social opportunities although she wasn't sure that's what this was. She slipped into some warm leggings and an oversized sweater plus a water resistant jacket and checked to make sure she had everything she needed in her small crossbody purse. At the last moment, she texted Mom in case Mom would call and she'd be gone. She saw Abby's mother's car slow down to a stop in front of their house. Sarah Jo ran out the door. No need for an umbrella – she'd outrun the raindrops!

Once in the restaurant, Sarah Jo shivered. The steamy warmth of it caused by the mingling of the various soup smells was delicious in itself. They sat down in the back, far from where the door could usher in cold air.

"That was nice of your mom to pick me up," said Sarah Jo.

"Well, your thanks to her pretty much covered that," said Abby. Her dark curly locks glistened in the dim light of the restaurant.

"I spose we should hurry and order. Your mom gave us an hour."

"What are you going to have, Sarah Jo?"

"I think I'll have tuna salad. How about you?" At that moment, a young man with an apron hastily tied around his waist, and a pen and pad in hand, approached their table.

"What'll it be, ladies?" Abby nodded in Sarah Jo's direction and the order taker focused on Sarah Jo.

"Tuna salad on toast and cream of leek soup, please."

"Great choice. And for you?" He looked in Abby's direction, pen poised at the pad.

"I think I'll have a Reuben. No soup."

"Anything to drink, either of you?" His name tag read Tim.

"I'll have some cocoa," said Abby.

"Just water for me," replied Sarah Jo, concluding the order. Tim turned on his heel and hurried away. "So, what did you want to tell me, Abby?"

"It's something kind of bad."

"What kind of bad?" asked Sarah Jo. "I mean there's bad and then there's *bad*.

"Well, it kind of has to do with Callie," she answered as the wait-person named Tim came back with their beverages.

"Watch out for the cocoa," he said as he set it down in front of Abby. "It's hot!"

"What do you mean it *kind of* has to do with Callie? In what way?"

"The other day I went to the library. I wanted to find a book to read for extra credit. I mean research I can do on my computer at home, but I kind of get my ideas for extra credit reports by browsing through the books themselves right at the library."

"Okay, so you were at the library *and...*?" Tim returned with their orders at the precise time Abby was going to answer.

"There you go. Now if you need anything, just let me know." He took off in a flash again.

"Abby, I don't know if an hour will be enough time to mine your story out of you," said an exasperated Sarah Jo.

"Well, that's not *my* fault. Anyway, I was between those tall shelves and I was about to go into the next aisle and I saw Austin and Callie sitting at a table a distance away."

"So? What's wrong with that?" Sarah Jo tasted her cream of leek soup. "Mmmmm."

"They were playing that game. The one with the spinner." Sarah Jo dropped her spoon.

"No! Really?"

"Yep," answered Abby as she took a bite of her sandwich.

"Abby, you know I'm not Callie's keeper, or Austin's for that matter."

"I know, but they were really engrossed in it, and Callie was writing things down after each spin."

"That part makes sense, writing each letter down – or number. So, what did you do?"

"Well, I didn't go over there by them if that's what you're thinking. I didn't want them to see me."

"Hmmm... guess that makes sense. I'd probably have done the same."

"Yes, and then I got out of there before either of them looked around."

"I don't know what to say except that it's interesting. I've never thought about the stuff that they do on their own. Callie never tells me anything. So, why did you decide to tell *me* about this?"

"I guess because I've never heard of that board game before, and I've never heard anything good about it from what *you've* told me," said Abby as she took her last bite of sandwich.

"Well, I'll have to think about this."

"Sarah Jo, if you decide to talk to either of them – or both – please don't mention *my* name."

"I won't Abby, but right now I'm not sure just what to make of this." The girls finished their lunches and paid and left their tips. Abby's mother would be there to pick them up soon.

***

After dinner Sarah Jo decided to go online. Whenever she needed information she usually did her research on the computer. She decided to put Spin and Win – or Not! into Search. She noticed that the results yielded little, if any, information about Austin's game. There was one entry that said it was a game manufactured by a company in the 1950s. The company was no longer in business.

"Hmmm..." she thought aloud. How would Austin have gotten his hands on a game from so long ago? "Maybe a family member? Or perhaps an antique store?" Maybe it didn't qualify as an antique but it could have just been an old item that people buy for nostalgia's sake. Oh well, she wasn't going to make a big deal out of it. For that matter, she had to wonder why Abby would drag her out into the rain to tell her something she could've mentioned over the phone. She probably was bored and just wanted to get together for lunch. Who knows?

Chapter Ten

Austin and Luke wanted to take Callie and Sarah Jo out on what, for all intents and purposes, might be called a date to make up for that horrible nightmare on Homecoming night after the dance – or so they said. Since it had already been mentioned, there was no reason *not* to follow through according to Austin. After giving it some thought, they decided to go to a roller rink in neighboring Brinksville. Dad gave it his full approval at dinner that night.

"Now that's an old fashioned date if ever there was one," he grinned. "I was pretty good at skating myself when I was a kid."

"Well, I'm *not,*" declared Sarah Jo. "I'm not so sure how ending up black and blue from falling is the definition of fun."

"You'll enjoy it dear," assured Mom, "once you get the hang of it. Just hold onto Luke's arm."

"Yeh, and then let go and fall, right?" retorted Sarah Jo. Mark stifled a laugh which caused everyone to look his way.

"*What?*" he asked innocently as he stabbed a piece of potato with gravy on it.

So the next day, Saturday, Luke picked Sarah Jo and the others up and they drove to Brinksville which was nine miles away.

"I suppose that dates at night are the usual thing, but I like the day-time better," said Sarah Jo.

"Well, after what happened after Homecoming, I'd say no one could blame you for feeling that way," said Austin. Luke nodded.

"If that hadn't happened at Burger Station, you'd feel differently, Sarah Jo."

"Exactly my point, Callie," replied Sarah Jo. They all ended up having a good time despite one fall that Sarah Jo predicted would happen. She wasn't hurt but it did knock the wind out of her.

"Hey, it's still early," said Austin. "Where should we go?"

"We could order some food from the Chicken Coop. I think they've got one here. We could take it to Rocky Ridges Park and have a picnic," said Callie.

"Well, I'm sure hungry," admitted Luke. "You'll get no resistance from me." So he drove to the Chicken Coop and took out a steaming box, that looked like a chicken coop, of fried chicken. The smell of it filled the car and they all were even hungrier by the time they arrived at the park. There was a picnic table with a view of the river and craggy rocks high above its banks. It wasn't long before the group was satisfied after having eaten two pieces each and biscuits with butter and honey.

"Now *that's* what I call a meal!" said Luke. "After all that skating, it really hit the spot." The girls, still working on theirs, nodded.

"Hey, I'll be right back," said Austin as he loped off, but not in the direction of the rest area. They wondered where he was off to; they guessed maybe to get a drink of water from one of the fountains in the park or something. In just minutes he reappeared with the all too familiar backpack on his shoulder. Sarah Jo groaned.

"Now *what?*"

"Hey, it's cool, guys. Let's do this one last time. I think I have enough data to come to a conclusion on how this thing works," said Austin.

"I think I'll pass," sighed Sarah Jo.

"You can't," said Austin. "You're needed here." He set up the board and got out his pen and pad. "Here Callie, you keep track of the letters, okay?"

"I suppose."

"Okay, let's start with Sarah Jo. Give it a spin." Sarah Jo complied, if grudgingly. The pointer stopped on the number nine. "Hey, that's weird."

"No kidding," exclaimed Callie. "I thought it only did that *after* a message."

"Usually it does," said Austin. "Try again." This time Sarah Jo spun a one.

"*What?*" said Callie. "This doesn't make sense."

"Let *me* try," said Callie. Her spin yielded another one.

"That's it. I'm done with this stupid experiment," said Sarah Jo, obviously annoyed. "I'd like to go home now. I've got *better* things to do." Austin looked crestfallen.

"Better do what the lady says," said Luke. Austin put the game away and they piled back into Luke's car.

"That game kinda ruined everything," said Callie, now ticked off. Luke drove out of the park and onto the highway.

"Gosh, I'm sorry," apologized Austin. "I didn't mean to mess up everyone's day."

"You maybe didn't, but I think your game had other ideas," said Callie.

"Let's change the subject," suggested Sarah Jo.

"Good idea," mumbled Luke. The light was fading as a thunderstorm approached. Luke turned on his lights. Just as he did, he saw something run across the road and it was big. He swerved to avoid it and ended up careening into the ditch on the other side. It was a steep ditch with craggy rocks below it. Because of the rocks, the car stopped short of the river. In the back seat Austin moaned in pain.

"Who's hurt?" demanded Luke. I know *you* are, Austin. Anyone else?" Sarah Jo was in front with Luke and was belted in securely.

"I'm okay," said Sarah Jo. "Callie?"

"I guess I am too, but my knees hurt where they hit the front seat."

"My leg feels like it's been broken," groaned Austin. "I just hope it isn't. That would really mess up basketball season."

"Quick," yelled Sarah Jo. "Someone call 9-1-1! I don't think this car is going to take us anywhere."

"I'll call," said Callie who finally got her replacement phone. After giving the details to dispatch, she dropped her phone. "Oh! My! God!"

"Hey Callie, I know you're upset but no need to take God's name in vain," said Sarah Jo.

"What did I just punch in?"

"I hope 9-1-1," said Austin.

"And what came up on that goofy game?" yelled Callie. "9-1-1!" They stared at one another wide-eyed.

"Just coincidence," said Austin finally.

"What- *really?*" said Callie.

"Aw c'mon, Callie," said Austin. You don't really believe that, do you?"

"I don't know what to believe."

"Look, I'm the one who's hurt here and I'm not blaming anyone – or *anything.* I mean if you want to lay blame, why not blame that creature that crossed the road in front of us?" Sirens were blaring in the distance and got louder as they approached.

"You know, I'd better call my parents," said Sarah Jo.

"Not yet," said Luke. "Wait till the paramedics and the sheriff gets here." The vehicles pulled to a stop at the top of the bank and the flashing lights reflected off the trees in the distance. The authorities edged their way down the bank, the paramedics with a board to load Austin onto. The sheriff and a deputy ordered them to stay in the car while they went to inspect the stability of it on the rocks.

"Okay, young man," said the sheriff to Luke. "Everything looks solid. You can come out." Luke unlocked his seatbelt and opened the door. He gingerly stepped out. In the meantime, the paramedics had opened the rear door and were examining Austin's leg.

"We won't know for sure what we have here until we get an X-ray of the leg. You'll have to be loaded on this gurney so we can take you to the hospital," said one of the paramedics.

"First, I need to get your name and then I need your parents' or guardian's name." Austin provided the needed information.

"The rest of you should be taken in also. Jim, check to see if they need basic medical help or if they can go in the cruiser. I'll need to see your drivers license and registration as well as your insurance card," the sheriff said as he nodded to Luke.

"They seem okay, Bob. They'll mainly end up with contusions."

"Okay, then we'll go to the hospital and Derek, you can get their information on the way back. I don't like the looks of this storm brewing. We'll deal with your car later, young man."

***

At the sheriff's department, Sarah Jo's parents were waiting as were Callie's and Luke's. The traces of concern that occupied their faces turned into relief upon seeing their teens. The sheriff immediately told the parents that the paramedics had assessed any possible injuries and they felt that it wasn't urgent that they go to the hospital immediately.

"However," said the sheriff, "I would recommend you parents take your young person in, just in case. They can stop by here later to give their version of what happened. I can see no crime has been committed here so I'm not going to hold them."

***

Although Sarah Jo protested, Mom and Dad insisted she go to the ER to be checked. The others ended up there too. It turned out that the only one with an injury was Austin; it was a sprain. The paramedic was right about other injuries, namely contusions which was bruising that had begun to make itself evident. In spite of the brewing storm, the parents figured they would take their respective children to the Sheriff's Department and get that over with. Austin was kept at the hospital since he wasn't allowed to put weight on his leg. He could go home in the morning when his foster parents would come and get him.

As anticipated, talking to the sheriff was routine. It was confirmed that the accident had been caused by an animal crossing the road since everyone had seen a flash of something crossing.

"You kids are darn lucky. That car could've gone all the way down the ravine and into the river. The insurance company probably won't like the fact that Austin swerved. They generally recommend just hitting the animal. Someone could've been coming from the other direction and things could've been a whole lot worse. Just swerving and losing control and going off the road is bad enough though."

***

The next day Abby called to get the story "straight from the horse's mouth," as Abby's father would say.

"What happened *this* time?" demanded her friend. Sarah Jo had to admit that it must look weird that things seemed to be happening on a regular basis.

"Well actually, I'm not sure," confessed Sarah Jo. "We went roller skating in Brinksville and -"

"Who's we?"

"Callie and Austin, and Luke and I."

"Thanks for inviting *me*," said Abby sarcastically.

"You're welcome, Abby. That coulda been *you* in the car along with us when we went down the embankment. Actually, this is all because we wanted to make up for what happened after Homecoming."

"Well, you sure outdid yourself this time, SJ."

"By the way, how did you find out about this?"

"My mom heard it from Luke's mother at the Senior Center where they volunteer. So, I get that you guys were at Rocky Ridges Park?"

"Yeh, we stopped at the Chicken Coop first and got takeout."

"Was it good?" asked Abby.

"Decent."

"Okay, so what else did you do. Just eat and then left for Pine Moor?"

"Well kinda.." Sarah Jo's voice trailed off.

"C'mon girl, spill. There's more to the story than that. I know you didn't go on a nature walk or back to the car for some extracurricular activity."

"Well, um, Austin had his game with -"

"Oh no, don't tell me! Oh my gosh – you *didn't!*"

"He said it was the last time in his experiment."

"Sarah Jo, didn't he say that *last* time?"

"Well uh..."

"You should've taken that creepy game and tossed it into the river."

"Yeh, but we were finished playing with it and Austin put it away. We didn't associate it with -"

"*What* - getting killed?"

"Oh come on, Abby. Don't be so dramatic."

"Sarah Jo, what kind of message did you get from it there?"

"We didn't, just some numbers."

"That doesn't make sense," said Abby. "This just keeps getting crazier all the time." Sarah Jo had to admit that it was confusing. For one thing, she didn't see this cross examination coming. No time to even think things through for herself, let alone someone demanding answers.

"Look Abby, let me think about what we've talked about and maybe see what Callie thinks; then I'll get back to you."

"See what Callie thinks? I think she's blind as a bat when it comes to Austin. Good luck!" she added sarcastically.

"Whatever," answered Sarah Jo who was now herself perturbed. Wouldn't be the first time that trouble swirled around that game. "Okay. Talk to you later." Tomorrow would be soon enough to talk to Callie. She had a project she was working on for a class called Current Events Solutions. Every month she was to choose a news topic that showed a problem in today's society. Then she was to do a report that gave her way of solving it. It wasn't easy, but she was solely in charge of figuring out the solution. Great, she thought, first she had to come up with something in the news and find a solution and then - boom! - she had to do the exact same thing in real life with this Spin and Win – or Not game. Well, at least it forced her to think even though she really wasn't in the mood to think about Austin's game.

***

"Sarah Jo," said Mom the next morning, which happened to be a very brisk fall day. "Do you think you could put together a stew for me for tonight? Everything's in the fridge – the beef, carrots and celery, plus there are onions and potatoes here on the counter. Just throw them into the slow cooker on low for the day."

"Sure, Mom." Before long, Sarah Jo had the house to herself and she would begin her day by delving into the Bible. Then she thought about the stew. Better take care of that first. She enjoyed cooking, but not today. She had a lot to do and making dinner was just one more thing. Sarah Jo put the beef stew meat in the bottom of the cooker, then layered the cut up potatoes, carrots, onions and celery on top. All the while she was thinking of a news item she might write her report about. She had just about finished assembling the stew when the phone rang. Before she did, she plugged in the slow cooker. There, that took care of that!

"Oh hi Cal. You're up early. I've been thinking about you."

"Good thinking or bad thinking?"

"Neither actually," answered Sarah Jo. "How's Austin doing?"

"Better. Good thing it was just a sprain and not something worse. He's home now, of course."

"Well, I'm glad it wasn't worse. It coulda been with his long legs. Luke's car isn't the roomiest."

"Yeh, I know."

"I'm kinda glad you called cuz I've been thinking about this whole thing. Did Austin ever tell you where he got that game, Callie?"

"Not really. He just said he picked it up somewhere."

"The *somewhere* is what I'm wondering about," commented Sarah Jo.

"I wouldn't worry about it," replied Callie. "There's enough to think about with school and the holidays coming."

"That's for sure," said Sarah Jo in agreement. "Well look, I've got to get going. Lots of schoolwork to get done today. Maybe we can talk later." At lunch, Sarah Jo was unpleasantly surprised to find out that although she'd plugged in the slow cooker, the dial was set on Off. Great, she thought. Everything was still cold. Now she'd have to jack up the heat to High to make up for lost time. She was annoyed at herself for making such a foolish mistake. This day had not gotten off to a very good start!

Chapter Eleven

Thanksgiving was fast approaching and Sarah Jo was looking forward to it. All the excitement had died down and it seemed her life at this point was drama-free. It was like she'd told Callie almost like a warning not to change things for her that she, Sarah Jo, was now living in a drama-free zone and she was lovin' it! In fact, the whole family was doing okay. Mark was now playing basketball and doing surprisingly well. But oddly, when it came to basketball, things were not going well at all with Austin or so Callie had told her. It was true that he'd only sprained his ankle from the accident at Rocky Ridges Park, but it gave him trouble from time to time. Basketball put a lot of strain on his ankle and it sometimes gave way during crucial plays. Coach usually pulled him from the game at that point. He'd been very patient with Austin but now was considering sidelining him for the season. It was in a near panic that Austin brought his plight before the church for prayer during the Prayer and Praise time near the end of the service.

"I'd like to ask for prayer for my ankle," said Austin to the congregation. "As you know, I was in an accident several weeks ago. I know that for those who've been aware of it, you've been praying. But now I may lose my position on the team because of the injury, so I'm asking for prayer that my ankle will heal so I don't have to leave." Sarah Jo felt bad for him. Right now her life was going so well she couldn't imagine having to deal with that. Sure, she and Callie and Luke ended up with bruises from the accident but certainly nothing life-changing.

A couple days later Sarah Jo heard from Callie. She wasn't prepared for what Callie told her. She said that Austin asked if she could meet him at the library after school. Callie could and did. What Austin had in mind came in the form of the ever-present backpack that accompanied him, it seemed, wherever he went. She didn't know for sure what Austin wanted so she decided to wait until he brought it up, and he did.

"'I have just one more thing I want to do with Spin and Win – or Not,' he said as he pulled the game out from his backpack. He laid it on the table before him. 'I need some answers and you can be my witness, Callie.' Then, to her surprise he mumbled, 'Show me if I'll remain on the team.' After that he began spinning the pointer."

"*What?*" blurted out Sarah Jo incredulously.

"I know!"

"What happened next, Callie?"

"Well, first of all, it just spun out gibberish; I mean one letter after another that had nothing to do with anything. It didn't make sense. I was about to walk away when Austin called out to me. 'Wait!' so I did. Then he told me it was making sense. He kept spinning until numbers came up, but he had the weirdest look on his face."

"What do you mean?"

"Well, he looked shocked and puzzled if you can imagine that."

"Did he say why?" asked Sarah Jo.

"Not exactly. He just pointed at what he'd written down."

"Well, what did it say?" demanded Sarah Jo.

"Just two words: you fail."

"You fail? What's *that* sposed to mean?"

"I don't know, Sarah Jo, but Austin sure didn't look happy.

"Then what happened?"

"He just said, 'I gotta get going' and took off.

"That's it?" asked Sarah Jo.

"Well, he turned around and said, 'See ya' and that was that."

"Wow..." said Sarah Jo. "Just wow."

Well, here was the drama that she was trying to avoid, thought Sarah Jo. She tried to conclude the conversation on a hopeful note but she wasn't sure she pulled it off successfully. She knew Callie cared for Austin, perhaps even too much. It seemed as though that backpack with its hitchhiker inside was an intruder. Now you're being silly, she thought. It's just a piece of cardboard with a metal spinner – just a game. The problem was, it seemed to have a hold on Austin. He sure gave it a lot of attention. The good thing was, Thanksgiving was right around the corner.

***

"Sarah Jo," said Mrs Foster to her daughter. "We have to think about the holidays, mainly Thanksgiving."

"Turkey day!" shouted out Mark, bounding down the stairs. "I can hardly wait."

"You're *always* hungry," said Sarah Jo. "We ought to have liver this year."

"*Liver*!? Who eats liver on Thanksgiving?"

"You would – if you were starving to death," replied Sarah Jo. "So Mom, aren't we having the usual?"

"Well, if that's what everyone wants. Get a paper and pen." Sarah Jo equipped herself accordingly as she sat down at the table.

"Okay, let's see, everyone wants turkey, right?

"I do, Mom," Mark was quick to reply. He grabbed an apple from the bowl in the center of the table and sat down also.

"Please write this down then, Sarah Jo. I'd like this to be a family effort this year."

"Maybe we ought to have the menfolk make the turkey," chuckled Sarah Jo.

"Hey yeh!" said Mark. "Can we cook it in a turkey fryer out on the driveway?"

"I think we've had this discussion before," reminded Mrs. Foster.

"If he's cooking, I'm not eating," declared Sarah Jo as she doodled on one corner of the paper.

"Good, all the more for the rest of us," retorted Mark, smiling.

"No need to worry, Sarah Jo. Now let's get back to the task at hand."

"Okay Mom, what's next?"

"What else do we usually have?" asked Mom.

"Stuffing?" volunteered Mark.

"I've already written that down," said Sarah Jo. "It's kind of part of the turkey."

"Okay then, how about mashed potatoes? And what about yams?"

"Good, Mark. We've got the potatoes covered," said Mom.

"I'm going to say that casserole with the green beans in it," said Sarah Jo.

"Hey, what's all this talk about food?" said Dad as he entered the kitchen with the folded newspaper under his arm. He took off his reading glasses.

"It's our Thanksgiving menu," said Mark. "They won't let us cook the turkey in case you're wondering, Dad."

"I wasn't. I just like to eat turkey, not cook it," said Mr. Foster. He got a glass of water and took it out with him to the family room.

"Now, let's see," said Mom, more to herself than anyone in the room. "Why don't we fix one fancy salad – like a fruit salad?" Sarah Jo wrote it down. Dessert, of course, would be pumpkin pie made from scratch. There were pie pumpkins yet in the garden that would be good for that, reminded Mom.

"Okay, so Mark here's your project. You can make a centerpiece appropriate for the season to go on our table. Don't make it too big though," cautioned Mom. "Our table will probably be filled to capacity with food and tableware."

"Isn't that women's work?"

"Women's work?" said Mrs. Foster and Sarah Jo simultaneously.

"Well, if you'd like to, you can clean the house instead. That work is hard enough for a boy your age. I want it done thoroughly though," said Mrs. Foster.

"Mommmm..." whined Mark. "I'll do the centerpiece."

***

Thanksgiving went off without a hitch and the food met everyone's expectations. Of course it wasn't all about the food, Dad reminded the Foster family. There was much to be thankful for this year and they all credited it to God for that outcome.

"Look at it this way," said Dad. "How much worse could it have been for you, Sarah Jo, with that accident? Your mother and I were praying all the way to the Sheriff's Department, weren't we, Peg?" Mom nodded vigorously.

"And what about you, Mark, when you took that tumble down the basement stairs?" added Mom.

"That's true," said Dad. "Plus that tree that was struck in the yard could have caused more serious consequences. I'd say we've been plenty blessed, don't you?" The family agreed.

"This turkey's really good, Mom," said Mark. "I'm glad Dad and I didn't get the job of cooking it."

"Now you're talking, son," Dad concurred as he helped himself to another slab of white meat. Throughout the meal, while the family enjoyed their good food and their blessings, Sarah Jo puzzled over the events of the past few months, especially those involving Austin. She knew he was having a good Thanksgiving, as were her other friends, but she couldn't help but wonder what was next for the poor guy. Although he'd asked for prayer from the congregation, he'd been temporarily sidelined and Sarah Jo detected a bitter attitude creeping in.

"You're awfully quiet, Sarah Jo. Is everything okay?" asked Mom.

"Oh sure, I just have a project on my mind."

"Well dear, do you think it will keep till tomorrow?" continued her mother as she lifted the gravy boat to pass to Mark who'd refilled his serving of mashed potatoes.

"Yes, it definitely will, Mom," replied Sarah Jo with a smile. No need to let a heavy duty issue spoil the day. But it kind of did. Confirmation of that came later when dinner was long over, the dishes cleaned up and the family was looking to make turkey sandwiches for themselves for the evening meal.

The phone rang and it was Callie.

"Happy Thanksgiving!" greeted Sarah Jo in a festive tone.

"Yeh, back at you," returned a breathless Callie. "Did you hear what happened to Austin? No, of course not! That's what I'm calling to tell you."

"What *happened?!*"

"Austin was having turkey dinner at his folks' place. He choked on a bite of turkey and nearly died!"

"*What?*"

"Yep, it was almost the end of Austin Reynolds. It was good his dad knew the Heimlich maneuver or this would be an entirely different conversation."

"Where is he now, at the hospital?"

"No, his parents wanted him to go, but he wouldn't. I guess they were just trying to do the responsible thing. They didn't want to get in trouble with the police."

"Well, I hope it was because they were concerned for *him.*"

"I'm sure it was, Sarah Jo. Nobody stopped to analyze motive at a time like that. I was just saying..."

"Well, all I can say is that's a horrible way to celebrate Thanksgiving, Callie."

"Really? I think it's something to really be *thankful* for – to be alive."

"You've got a point there, Cal."

***

Before bed that night, Sarah Jo decided to try and piece things together regarding Austin. First of all, she wasn't going to tell her parents about him choking, at least not for now. She wondered why all these things kept happening to him. He was new in the faith so some of that was not unusual. But to be at the point of death – what was *that* about? She put on her pajamas and brushed her hair. She yawned. It had been a long day and it didn't take long to drift off to sleep.

Suddenly, Sarah Jo bolt upright in her bed! She looked at the clock on the nightstand. It had been about three hours since she went to bed.

Her heart was beating hard in her chest. What had awakened her was a nightmare – and the realization that Austin might well be playing with fire! She turned on the light. There, that helped. Everything began to make sense now. She got up and sat at her desk. It was time to ask the hard questions - now!

Could it be...? She walked the question back and started over. Could it be that unbeknownst to Austin he was calling upon wrong spirits connected with that game? She couldn't remember anything good happening as a result of that game and its answers. The first time was when Laura had those salty waffles after the cookout/sleepover when Austin brought his game that night. Of course, that could have been coincidence at Mark's hand as he played a prank when he put extra salt in Laura's waffles. The second time was when she, Callie and Abby were going clothes shopping and having lunch when Austin showed up there. That's when he said he wanted to experiment with the game. The message that time was: *you are in trouble.*

It was true! That game predicted – actually predicted – nothing but trouble! Even when they were at the park it used numbers to predict its dire warning: 9-1-1! It sent chills down her spine. If this was true, then they were in more trouble than they had bargained for. Sarah Jo needed to talk to Austin – and she didn't want that game anywhere near her again. She'd call him later. Because it was the Friday after Thanksgiving, he'd be on vacation. She went back to bed reluctantly. How could she sleep now? She was still tired from yesterday's festivities and fell asleep again readily. When she woke up, the sun was shining brightly and she recalled her realization about Austin and that game. It was time to get up and put her plan into action. She decided to call Austin first thing.

"Hi Austin, it's me - Sarah Jo."

"Yeh, your voice sounded familiar. What's up?"

"How are things with you? Callie told me last night that you choked or something yesterday."

"Uhh yeh, bad news travels fast I guess."

"What happened?"

"Well, I was just eating dinner with my parents and this bite of turkey got stuck in my throat so my dad came over and did the Heimlich maneuver on me. It popped right out. I have to admit it was pretty scary."

"Wow! I'm sure it was," said Sarah Jo.

"I have to say, Thanksgiving dinner didn't taste so good after that."

"Well, I'm just glad your dad knew what to do and that you're still around."

"Yeh, me too."

"Hey Austin, do you think you could meet for cocoa or something, like maybe at Connie's?"

"When?"

"I don't know, maybe in a couple of hours?"

"Sure, I guess so. I gotta run right now, but I'll see you at one there, okay?"

"Sounds good, Austin. See you then."

***

As Sarah Jo made her way over to Connie's Cocoa Cottage, she thought about Austin and the situation. It was more than troubling; it was downright mysterious, but she would solve the mystery one way or the other. She felt now that Austin was in actual danger in a way most people wouldn't consider. But why? Why did it seem to be linked to that game and why now? She planned to find out. She never thought of herself as a reporter on the trail of a story, but now she would do what she had to in order to get answers. When she got to Connie's, Austin was already there standing next to his bike.

"Hi Sarah Jo," he greeted her. "You decided to walk?"

"Oh sure. It's not that far. It's good exercise." They entered Connie's and ordered their mugs of steaming cocoa topped with mini marshmallows.

"So, Sarah Jo, to what do I owe the honor of this meet up?"

"Well, first of all, how have you been; I mean *really* been?

"Hmm... you answered my question with a question. Well, okay, since you asked, not so great."

"I kind of figured. I just want to clue you in on something. Remember when you asked the church for prayer a few weeks back?" Austin nodded. "Well, Callie told me you checked with 'Mr. Wizard' of Spin and Win – or Not! fame. She said you asked if you'd be able to play on the team."

"Yeh, so what of it? And by the way, do you and Callie always make me the center of discussion?"

"No Austin, I have plenty to do without playing guessing games about your life," said Sarah Jo. Actually though it kind of was what she'd been doing lately and for good reason.

"Well, why did you ask then?"

"For one thing, it's not a good idea to go to God by asking for prayer and then turn to something else for the answer, well, except if it's the Bible."

"So what are you saying, Sarah Jo, that you think I asked the congregation for prayer for no good reason?"

"Not at all, Austin. I'm just saying when you go to God – even through someone else by asking for prayer – you've gone to the *top*. It doesn't get any better, or higher, than that. It's kind of an insult to God to look to Him for help and then go to that goofy game for an answer."

"Well, I don't know if I'd call it goofy, but in any case, no harm done."

"Or so you think," said Sarah Jo. Connie bustled over to their booth with a carafe of hot cocoa.

"Ready for a refill?" she asked. "I saw you in the middle of a deep discussion so I didn't want to interrupt."

"I'll pass on the refill for now," said Sarah Jo. Austin held out his cup. Connie had a small bag of mini marshmallows in her apron pocket and deposited a few on top. "Call me when you're ready, Sarah Jo."

"Look, Sarah Jo, as much as I appreciate your concern for me, I don't need a guilt trip on top of everything else."

"Austin, don't be so sensitive. I care about you and so do Callie and the others. If you want to fault us for something, then do it because of the fact that we care. I have a question for you." Austin looked up from inspecting his cocoa. "Where exactly did that game come from?"

"I don't know," he answered. "At least not exactly."

"How about a clue then." Austin took a long, slow sip from his cup.

"You probably aren't going to like this." He looked up. "We had a silent auction at the Fellowship and.."

"You mean your so-called church at the time."

"Whatever," he replied, the annoyance surfacing in his voice. "Anyway, I was the highest bidder and I got the game."

"Couldn't have been too high a bid. It's just cardboard and metal."

"True, but it belonged to Fern Samuels."

"How do you know?"

"Cuz she walked by after I won it and said that she was glad that I had gotten it and that it had belonged to her mother."

"What – *really?* Did she say anything else?"

"Yeh, she just said she hoped that I had as much fun with it as she and her sister did when they were kids."

"What kind of fun would that be – the kind you've been having lately?"

"What are you implying, Sarah Jo, that none of that was coincidence? I mean accidents *do* happen."

"No, I'm not implying that," said Sarah Jo. "I'm telling you *outright* that that's exactly what I think."

"I think we're done here," said Austin as he got up from the booth.

"Wait Austin, I think there's something you should know. Please sit down."

"What more is there to discuss, Sarah Jo?" Austin slowly sat back down in the booth.

"A lot more than you obviously know about," she answered. "As a Christian sister I'm going to give you a choice."

"A choice?"

"Yes. That you either listen to me about this or go to Pastor Martin and hear it from him."

"Hear *what?*"

"Back as promised," said Connie as stopped at the booth. "Well, maybe I didn't promise, but refills are as good as promised to my customers. Want some more cocoa?"

"I'll take some now," said Sarah Jo. Connie poured.

"How about you?" she asked Austin.

"Sure. Thanks."

"You're welcome," said Connie smiling, then she bustled off.

"Okay, so where were we?" asked Austin.

"Choices," answered Sarah Jo.

"About what? Why are you being so mysterious?"

"I'm not. I've always been upfront with you." She could already detect the influence of that game on Austin.

"Okay, let me hear it from *you*, Sarah Jo."

"You got it!" She was glad that her silent prayer had been heard.

Chapter Twelve

Yesterday had seemed like a dream to Sarah Jo. Her "mission" was accomplished with Austin but now she didn't know what he'd do with the information she gave him. For her, today was like any other Saturday. For Austin it would not be. Maybe she should've let Pastor Martin handle it. Well, even now she could still recommend Austin go and talk with him, especially if he had any questions.

She pictured Austin sitting across from her at Connie's staring wide-eyed as she told him things he'd never heard before. It wasn't long before his brows had knit together and his forehead creased with concern.

"So you see, Austin," she'd said, "just as there is the invisible – but very real - world of God and His angels, there is also the unseen world of the devil and his spirits."

"So what are you saying then, that I've been dealing with the wrong world?" He poked at the marshmallows with his spoon.

"Yeh, pretty much. Well, not that you've been looking to do it, but you left yourself open to it and they're quick to accommodate."

By the time they were done, Sarah Jo felt she'd gotten through to Austin. She hoped he understood what all she'd told him. If she'd had any doubts, there was a confirmation today at church of that knowledge she'd shared with him. That fact alone told her that timing is crucial with God. Pastor Martin's sermon was on that very subject and she hadn't even mentioned it to him!

"So, my brothers and sisters in the Lord, although I've spoken on this subject before, I feel it's necessary to once again bring it up. Now we're not to be afraid of the Enemy, but neither are we to be ignorant of his devices as it says in the Bible. He will come after you in various ways, but the Lord is infinitely stronger than the Enemy is." As Pastor Martin preached, Sarah Jo looked in Austin's direction but there was little she could tell by the expression on his face. He just looked like he was taking it all in like he did with Pastor's every sermon.

"That was *some* sermon Pastor Martin preached today," said Dad at lunch. "What did all of you think?" He reached for another sloppy joe. Sarah Jo had to admit she and Mom had outdone themselves on preparing this fairly simple lunch.

"I think you're absolutely right, dear," said Mom. "It's probably one that should be preached at *least* once a year."

"Yeh," chimed in Mark. "It's kinda creepy, but I like that kind of sermon."

"Creepy?" questioned Dad. "I don't see it that way. Creepy is when a person doesn't have faith in Jesus Christ as their personal Saviour. Now *that's* creepy!"

"Dad, I think most people believe in the halloween type of creepy. It's almost like they *want* to be scared of witches, skeletons and ghosts and things," said Sarah Jo.

"Well, those things can be creepy too, as you kids put it," admonished Dad. "But they don't have the power, of and by themselves, to rob a person of eternity."

"What I find interesting is that a skeleton is like a symbol of fear to most people; hopefully not Christians," said Mom. "Can you imagine how we human beings could function without a skeleton?"

Sarah Jo and Mark looked at each other, then burst into laughter.

"I know it sounds funny," said Dad, "but your mother is absolutely right."

***

That afternoon Sarah Jo decided to call Callie. She wanted to tell her about her meeting with Austin. She'd rather Callie hear it from her than Austin. She believed the Troublemaker was already at work with Austin; she'd seen it in his attitude.

"Hi SJ," said Callie. "What's up?"

"Are you busy right now?"

"Nope, we just got done with lunch."

"Same here," said Sarah Jo. "Wanna go to the park for awhile? It won't be long before it's too cold."

"Sure, I can get away in about fifteen minutes. How about I meet you in a half hour or so?"

"Okay," said Sarah Jo. "Let's meet at the gazebo end of the park." That way she knew they wouldn't run into Austin should he decide to shoot a few hoops. She put on a fleece hoodie knowing she might get too warm in it, but then again she might get cold later. As she walked along in the direction of the park she decided how she'd tell Callie about her talk with Austin. It wasn't that big of a deal. Callie knew about the devil and his tactics, but still, it wasn't their everyday type of conversation. She saw Callie in the distance – at least she thought it was her – sitting on a park bench. Upon getting closer, she *knew* it was her; a wave from Callie confirmed it.

"Hey Sarah Jo."

"Hi Callie. Guess I could've talked to you in church this morning but it's hard to with everyone around. Let's sit on a bench in the gazebo." They made their way over to it.

"Good sermon, huh? A little strange maybe but I guess Pastor thought it was probably timely."

"Yeh, I think he mentioned it was time for it. So have you talked to Austin lately?" She watched a green leaf with tinges of orange float listlessly to the ground.

"Nothing more than hi and bye. Why do you ask?"

"Because I have. I asked if he could meet me yesterday at Connie's."

"Why? Are you wanting to steal my guy?" Callie asked jokingly.

"I didn't know he was yours," retorted Sarah Jo with mock surprise.

"He's not. But I *do* like him."

"So do I. Maybe not the way you do, but I'm concerned for him."

"In what way, SJ?"

"Well, I think that game of his is somehow connected to wrong spirits."

"You mean *demons?*"

"Don't act so shocked, Callie. You've known about them for a long time. Maybe not in connection to Austin, but still..."

"No, I've never associated them with him. Why would I?"

"Well, mainly cuz of that game. Can you think of one good thing that has come after playing it? And what about its messages?" So they replayed the history of the messages and the events that followed, none of them good.

"Wowww..." said Callie.

"Right?" confirmed Sarah Jo. Callie nodded, wide-eyed. "So I asked Austin where he got the game from. Know what he said?" Callie shook her head. "He said he got it from a church – cult – event at a silent auction. He won it at that auction. Then Fern Samuels congratulated him on his winning it saying she hoped he had as much fun with it as she and her sister did as kids."

"From *whom* did you say?"

"Fern Samuels. Remember her?" asked Sarah Jo acidically.

"I heard you right; just wish that I hadn't. She's an evil woman!"

"I'd say!"

"Well, I don't know for sure, but she might have demonic stuff way back in her family history. All I know is that she's bad news!"

"The point is that Austin may be playing with fire and not even know it," said Sarah Jo.

"Well, I can tell you that he'd never do it knowingly."

"Maybe not, Callie, but he's become rather defensive lately when it comes to that game." In the distance, kids' laughter came from the area of the playground.

"So, what can *we* do about it?"

"I'm not sure. If it is what I suspect, the Enemy will not like us trying to break up Austin and his game. You know the devil likes to control."

"Yeh, but if it *is* the Enemy, he could cause a lot of trouble, right?

"A *lot* of trouble, yes," confirmed Sarah Jo.

"Well, maybe we should take it to Pastor, do you think?"

"Not just yet," said Sarah Jo. "But you could kind of keep your eye out on Austin now that you know what's going on."

"In what way? Am I sposed to be his keeper now?" She could see the kids playing now, through the lattice of the gazebo. They looked like they were having great fun scampering around.

"Of course not, silly. That's our Lord's job. But you can be on the lookout. You're in the best position to do that."

"Okay, well then tell me what to be looking for."

"My goodness, Callie! You have the Holy Spirit, and you also know how the devil works. He's crafty. He'll catch you off guard. One of those moments is bound to creep in at some point, I'd say."

"Hey, you're scaring me, SJ. I don't want the Enemy hanging out around *me*." Sarah Jo noticed the desperate sound in her voice.

"Nobody in their right mind does; I mean a believer anyway. I'm just saying that if you notice anything unusual, let me know. In this case, two heads are better than one."

"Okay, will do. Well, I've gotta get going – if I even make it home in one piece." Callie fake grimaced.

"Callie, you are something else! You have the Holy Spirit, as I said before. You know the devil flees just at the sound of Jesus' name."

"Yeh, I guess you're right. But just the same I don't need all this drama."

"Neither does Austin and we're going to help him out if we can." Sarah Jo raised her fist to invite Callie to a fist bump. They would be fighting this together.

Chapter Thirteen

"You look deep in thought, Sarah Jo," said Dad at dinner, glancing at his daughter.

"Don't let that fool you, Dad," offered Mark. "Looks can be deceiving." He chuckled; his parents did not.

"Mark, that was uncalled for," scolded Mom. "There's nothing wrong with thinking. More people should do it – especially before they speak."

"Ouch!" said Mark. "Um, would someone please pass the potatoes?"

"Certainly, son," said Dad as he passed the snowdrift of mashed potatoes to his son. Sarah Jo didn't feel like being questioned about what she was focusing on at the moment. It didn't make sense to talk about something even *she* didn't understand. If Austin had hooked into the demonic realm there was no telling what he'd be dealing with.

"Oh, I'm just thinking about the day, Dad," answered Sarah Jo finally.

"Anything exciting happen, dear?" asked Mom, taking a bite of chicken.

"Well, not really. I mean I met up with Callie at the park. It won't be long before it gets too cold to do that."

"I agree," said Dad. "Winter is just around the corner. We just got a late fall blessing with *this* weather."

"So, how is she doing?" pursued Mom.

"Well, as far as I can tell, she's doing okay. Why?"

"No reason. Just interested in you – and your friends." Mark downed a whole glass of milk.

"Better you than me," he said and then burped loudly. "Excuse me."

"I've been trying to," quipped Sarah Jo.

"Funny," said Mark. "In fact, so funny I forgot to laugh. May I be excused?"

"Sure," said Dad, "but take your plate, glass and silverware and rinse them off and put them in the dishwasher, would you?"

"Yep."

"How about 'yes Dad' or 'yes sir'?"

"Yes sir, Dad." Mark scrambled to clear his place at the table.

"So, Sarah Jo, Callie's doing okay then?" Mom looked at her intently.

"Well, no one's life is perfect."

"Maybe not; we all have to deal with problems from time to time."

"Not *this* kind of problem, though." Sarah Jo immediately regretted letting that escape.

"What kind of problem, daughter?" asked Dad. Suddenly Sarah Jo lost her appetite.

"Um... it's kind of private," she said barely audibly. That was just the red flag Dad needed.

"I'd like to know what this about. If it involves you it involves us as your parents." Mom nodded.

"Well, Austin carries this game around with him. It's just a piece of junk actually, no big deal."

"And that's what *this* is all about?" asked her father.

"Well, kinda."

"Kinda what, Sarah Jo?"

"He likes for us to play it when we all get together. It's just kind of a corny game."

"Tell me what kind of a game it is. How does it work?"

"Dad it's no big deal. It's a word game. It's just that some of the stuff it spells is weird."

"In what way?" demanded Dad.

"I don't know, just telling us stuff that might happen or something." Dad rubbed his chin as if in deep thought.

"Sounds like a ouija board to me. Is that what it is?"

"No, Dad. It isn't that kind of game. This has a spinner on it." Sarah

Jo didn't want to tell her parents how central this game had been to their lives lately – or where it came from.

"Sarah Jo! I'm surprised at you. The devil doesn't need a particular board game to wield his influence. Even the common horoscope column in the paper can be used to his advantage. I think there's a real problem here and I intend to get to the bottom of this."

"Yes, Dad."

"We're here to help you, honey," said Mom. "God isn't going to have you give up anything that's good for you."

"Who said it's not good?" argued Sarah Jo. "It's not *my* game anyway."

"Have you played it?" asked Mom.

"Well, sort of…"

"Sort of?" asked Dad.

"I just mean that when Austin's brought it around, the group of us has played it. Austin is doing an experiment with it to see if it's on target with predicting stuff."

"What is the name of this game," asked Dad, as he drummed his fingers on the table.

"It's called Spin and Win – or Not!"

"I don't like the sound of that. It's the 'or Not' part that concerns me." A worried look on Mom's face confirmed that she was in agreement.

"It's really just an old board game, Dad – better than some of the video games they've got out."

"Well, like I said, I'm going to get to the bottom of this one way or the other. It doesn't matter if it's old or not. Satan is older than both types of games." And that was dinner. Sarah Jo had no appetite for dessert; she'd hardly finished what was on her plate. She just wished she hadn't let slip mentioning that game. Dumb mistake, she chided herself. Dumb mistake!

***

Things weren't going well for Austin according to Callie in a phone conversation the next day. Sarah Jo was the first one she told about it. He had an attitude, as Callie put it. He was showing signs of bitterness, she told Sarah Jo.

"What does he have to be bitter about? I'd say life's been pretty good to him."

"Apparently, he doesn't see it that way. He never used to complain like he does now."

"What does he say, Callie?" She shifted her position on her bed. This would be a long call.

"Well, for one thing he says it wasn't so bad in that fellowship he used to be in, and that life was much simpler then."

"You're kidding!"

"I'm not kidding!" Callie contradicted.

"Do you know what that sounds like? Remember when the Israelites had left Egypt and after awhile they complained about how good they had it there?"

"Yeh, that's in the Old Testament."

"Doesn't matter; truth is truth. That part of the Bible was written for us to learn from too."

"So, what's your point, Sarah Jo?"

"Well, do you remember how they complained about the manna and wished for the food back in Egypt?"

"Yeh, I guess."

"Well, God gave them what they wanted – a bunch of quail! The Israelites made gluttons out of themselves eating all those birds."

"Okay..." Callie's voice trailed off.

"Then they got sick – really sick!"

"Okay, so you're comparing Austin to the Israelites? Is he sposed to get sick or something?"

"I don't know," said Sarah Jo. "It might turn out much worse than that. Austin should know better. So what do you tell him when he talks like that?"

"What *can* I say? I mean it's just his opinion. I have nothing to compare with. I just told him that his life seems okay."

"And he drops the subject?" Sarah Jo pulled on the fringe of her blanket at the end of the bed.

"Well, he sure didn't when I talked to him last night."

"What did he say?"

"Well, to quote him he said, 'I thought Christians were supposed to have the abundant life.'"

"So, he doesn't think he has that?" asked Sarah Jo.

"Guess not. He launched into a tirade about his ankle and how it's affected his playing basketball." Sarah Jo let out a long sigh. This didn't sound good – at all.

"Well, the blessings come from God, not the Enemy."

"You're preaching to the choir, as they say. I already know that."

"Cal, I think it's time for a visit to our pastor. This is serious."

"Good idea. I totally agree."

"I'll call Pastor tomorrow and set up a time. Is there any time that's *not* good for you?"

"Any time is fine, SJ. I don't have anything planned."

"If he asks me about a time, would Saturday work for you?"

"Yep, that's fine. Afternoon works best for me. I might sleep in."

"Okay. I'll call you tomorrow then or maybe text, okay?" Sarah Jo was glad she got that out of the way. She didn't want this dark cloud hanging over her or Callie's heads, and certainly not Austin's. The thing was, she felt partly responsible for him because she knew more about how the Enemy works than he did. She remembered Fern Samuels had said that they only tried to emphasize the positive in their group, and didn't "give place to the devil", as mentioned in the Bible. Sarah Jo felt that might be taking liberties with scripture on the part of Fern Samuels but she wasn't going to argue with her. But as she thought about it, she felt that maybe that was a clever way for the Enemy to protect himself. After all, with knowledge there is power.

✳✳✳

Sarah Jo decided to call Pastor Martin first thing that next morning.

She had slept a bit later and now it was nine o'clock, not too early to call. He would be in his office.

"Hi, Pastor? This is Sarah Jo Foster. Have you got a few minutes?" He did. She began to explain briefly Austin's situation.

"Sarah Jo, may I cut in for a moment?"

"Sure," she replied. It was almost like he knew what she was going to say.

"Why don't you invite Austin to come with you and meet with me down here at the church?"

"I could ask. I'm not sure if he'd go though. Also, would it be okay for Callie to come too?"

"I really don't think that would be wise. He might feel uncomfortable if he felt outnumbered."

So, now they had a plan. All she had to do was convince Austin to go along with it. She had a feeling that wasn't going to be easy. For all she knew, he might put up a big fight. Surprisingly though, he went along with it. Maybe he had been searching for answers. He *did* have the Holy Spirit, after all.

***

Austin was at the church when Sarah Jo arrived. She saw his bike outside the building, probably one of his last rides in the chill of the early December air. She shivered. It had been cold for her to walk but figured it would be helpful in meeting her Phy Ed requirements. She was met with a gust of warm fragrant air as she stepped in the door. Her church always smelled so good, like cinnamon. Sarah Jo made her way to Pastor Martin's office; the door was open.

"Come in, come in," said Pastor Martin as he stood up. "How are you today?" Austin craned his head around to see her and started to stand, but Pastor Martin motioned them both to sit down as he pointed to a chair for Sarah Jo.

"I'm fine, thank you. It's kind of getting cold out there," she said. "Pretty soon everything's going to be white."

"So true," agreed the pastor. "So true." He sat down behind his humble desk, one that had obviously been used for many years, and folded his hands together. "So, what can I do for you two?" Sarah Jo and Austin glanced at each other. Sarah Jo was first to speak.

"We've got a little problem here, Pastor." It was mostly Austin's but she wanted it to look like they were in this together. "I know this may sound funny, but there's this board game. Maybe Austin can explain it better." Austin shifted in his chair.

"Well uh, it's just a game I got at a silent auction. Sometimes I bring it with me when we get together."

"Who is *we?* asked Pastor Martin.

"Well, you know; friends that I know from here like Sarah Jo and Callie and others."

"Seems harmless to me," said the minister.

"That's what I thought too," said Austin. Sarah Jo hoped he would be totally open and honest about the game.

"But...?" Pastor leaned over in Austin's direction.

"Well, it's just that sometimes after we use it strange things seem to happen," replied Austin. Sarah Jo breathed an inner sigh of relief. He *was* going to tell it like it is.

"Strange things? Like what?"

"Well, Sarah Jo here seems to think these coincidences are linked to the game," said Austin nodding in her direction. Darn it! thought Sarah Jo, the Enemy was turfing it off on her and making her look like she was imagining this.

"They're pretty serious things, Pastor," said Sarah Jo. "It all started out harmlessly enough, like a joke being played, but recently linked to Mark's fall down the stairs and the accident with the car – the one which just happened to injure Austin's ankle."

"So you're saying you believe that this game is tied in with these events, Sarah Jo?"

"Yes Pastor, I am. It's happened too consistently to be coincidence."

"I see," said Pastor Martin thoughtfully. "Well, I think I'd better take a look at that game. Austin, do you think you could bring it with you to church? Afterward the three of us can sit down together and see if we can get to the bottom of this. I'd appreciate it if the two of you keep this is your prayers, as I will be."

The next day, Sunday, Sarah Jo and Austin met with Pastor Martin in his office. Austin had his board game with him, tucked discreetly into his backpack.

"What do you say we take out that game of yours and have a look, Austin," said Pastor Martin. He inspected the box and then opened it up. "Hmm... I haven't heard of this company before, nor have I ever seen such a game as this. It's probably on its way to being an antique."

"I guess it was in someone's family for years," volunteered Austin, breaking the silence.

"Okay, so after reading what directions there are, I think I understand how this thing works. From what I understand, it would make a good device for the Enemy to use in order to convey messages to the, uh, players – or shall I say *unsuspecting* players; much like a ouija board. Very clever; the Enemy is very clever indeed."

"Would you say this is risky to play then, Pastor?" Sarah Jo had to ask so that Austin would know. She herself would not touch such a game after all she'd seen happen.

"Oh absolutely!" declared their pastor. "I'd say burn it and be done with it." Austin opened his mouth as if to protest and then looked as though he had thought better of it.

"I'll take care of it," Austin said sensibly. Pastor Martin put the game back in its box and handed it back to him.

"Son, the sooner you get rid of this the better."

"See Austin," said Sarah Jo as they walked out of the church together. "The Enemy can even use a hunk of cardboard like that game to influence people."

"Yeh, I guess so, but it doesn't seem like he'd waste his time on us."

"Well, that's just the thing though. He wants to influence us at an early age so that it'll mess up our lives." Austin looked doubtful so Sarah Jo added, "I mean why wouldn't he want to get people when they're young and impressionable? Look at your situation. You were born into

     Barbara Ann Philleo

the organization that your parents were in, so it was logical that you'd adopt the views they believed in. I mean the same is true with regular church as well."

"I spose. Well, I'd better get going. I gotta get home. Bye Sarah Jo." He got onto his bike and pedaled off. Sarah Jo started off in the direction of home.

Chapter Fourteen

That night as she sat at her computer, Sarah Jo thought about something she'd spent little time on lately – college. She'd been so immersed in Austin's situation that she realized she hadn't been focusing on her own life that much. Even at dinner, the conversation centered around Austin and that game. She had decided to share the meeting she'd had with Pastor Martin, Austin and herself with her parents and, because he was at the dinner table too, with Mark.

"I *knew* there was something screwy about that game," Mark declared.

"How much do you know about it, you little wiseguy?" asked Sarah Jo.

"Hey, what do you think God gave me ears for, sis? You don't see earrings hanging off of them like with yours. My ears are dedicated listening devices."

"Mark, if you knew anything about ears you'd realize that the ears themselves mainly scoop up the sound waves. It's what's inside that completes the process."

"Hey you two," said Dad, his voice raised. "Enough!" Mom finished out the discussion by saying she felt Pastor Martin's advice was very wise.

"Better to be safe than sorry," she said. "There are better board games out there."

***

It was the very next morning that Sarah Jo had gotten the news. Austin was in trouble again. Callie notified her in no uncertain terms that Austin had taken things too far this time.

"What are you talking about, Callie?" asked Sarah Jo into the phone.

"Look, sorry for calling so early but I *had* to talk to you."

"No problem. Mom and Dad left for work and Mark is at school. What's going on?" She sat down with her cup of herb tea and prepared for the worst. Sarah Jo thought this issue was settled. She'd planned to call Callie this afternoon and tell her how things went with her and Austin's meeting with Pastor Martin.

"You won't believe Austin," said Callie. Sarah Jo noted the annoyance in her voice. "He stopped by last night and we went for a walk. It didn't take long before I figured out what he was interested in."

"*What?*"

"Yep, you heard me right. He made moves on me."

"That doesn't sound like Austin at all. He's not that way."

"Well, he was last night. I mean he wanted a hug and a kiss, but he knows I'm not into that. He always realized that what we have at this point is friendship."

"That doesn't make sense, Callie. I mean he knows where you're coming from. What did you say to him?"

"I told him that if that's what he's looking for to go somewhere else."

"And...?"

"Then he morphed into his old self again and apologized all over the place."

"Doesn't that work for you, Cal?"

"Sarah Jo," replied Callie impatiently, "it never should have happened in the first place."

"Yeh, I see your point." What had happened between yesterday's meeting after church with Pastor Martin and Austin's visit with Callie? She filled Callie in on the meeting with Pastor Martin which made Callie even more irritated with Austin.

"He should've known better, after what you said was discussed, SJ."

"He *should* have, but for some reason he didn't. Hey look, Cal, I've got a day's school work ahead of me, so I think I'd better get going."

"Yeh, hey, sorry to have bothered you, but something isn't right with Austin."

"Well, let me know if you find out anything more, okay Cal?"

"Will do," she promised.

***

Sarah Jo delved into her studies and was making good progress. It was almost lunch time when she heard a knock at the door.

"Now what?" she mumbled to herself. Did Callie have more information on the situation that just couldn't wait? She opened the door without thinking, only to see Austin standing there.

"Austin, what are *you* doing here? You're supposed to be in school."

"Well I, uh, sorta skipped."

"*What?* How come?"

"Umm, can I come in? It's kinda cold out here."

"I'm not sure, Austin. It's like you're a stranger these days. But come on in. I won't leave you standing out in the cold." Austin eased in, looking uncomfortable. She motioned to a chair in the living room. "So, what's going on?" Austin sat and looked down at the floor. "Well?"

"I've got some big problems and I don't know what to do."

"Problems like what?"

"Well, for one thing – that game."

"What's the problem *there?* Pastor Martin advised you on that – or did I just imagine that?" Sarah Jo was starting to lose patience with him. Austin moved to the edge of the chair.

"No, of course it wasn't your imagination."

"Well, did you?" pressed Sarah Jo. "Take his good advice, I mean?"

"Uh no – at least not yet anyway."

"Austin! No wonder you're nervous. You're playing with fire! I'd be nervous too."

"Well uh.." stammered Austin.

"What is so hard about destroying a piece of cardboard?"

"Could I – uh – have some water, please, Sarah Jo?" She brought the glass of water back, still stunned by the fact that he'd completely ignored Pastor Martin's wise advice.

"Why didn't you follow through on Pastor's advice, Austin?"

"Well, I just wanted to make sure."

"Of what exactly?"

"Well, that it was the right thing for me to do. You gotta remember that the outfit I was in, I had to follow orders to the letter – all the time. My parents made sure, and their authority was basically the same as the bishop's."

"Soooo...?"

"So I'm not so trusting this time around. I never even wanted to see the inside of a church again."

"Well, excuse me, Austin, but yours wasn't a church. It's called a cult, and by the grace of God you were set free."

"Whatever." Austin's ungrateful attitude was another shock to her. He had really changed.

"All right, so tell me what's wrong that you're all upset about."

"Well, I checked with the game this morning to see what the outcome will be for my basketball career. What it told me wasn't good."

"Like what?" Sarah Jo decided to play along without being judgmental for the moment.

"It said, in not so many words, that Pastor Martin is praying against me."

"*What?!*" exclaimed Sarah Jo incredulously. "Do you really believe that?"

"Why wouldn't I? It happened once before in Future Life Fellowship."

"Didn't you hear a word I said?" asked Sarah Jo. "That was *not* a church."

"Well, I know *you* believe that."

"So did you, Austin. What changed your mind?" Austin stood up and paced distractedly across the living room floor.

"I don't know. It just seems that I'm not to have a basketball career, for one thing. Why would God give it to me and then take it away?"

"Has it occurred to you that in a sense you perhaps took it away from yourself when you began messing with that game? It's almost like it's an authority to you – sort of like a god, and you know what God has to say about false gods. It's in the Bible, first commandment."

"Well, I can't take any chances."

"*Chances?* You already have. It sounds like you're threatening God. That's the biggest chance you've taken already."

"Sarah Jo, not everyone is as – as perfect as you."

"I can't believe what you're saying, Austin. I don't think that's you talking. Someone's putting wrong ideas into your heart and mind."

"I think I know what you're implying, so whatever we had – friendship or who knows what – it's done!" Austin headed toward the door and let himself out and slammed the door behind him.

***

Sarah Jo sat on the couch in shock. The slamming of the door reverberated in her mind. She should've realized what was happening. Now she needed to contact Pastor Martin again and get his advice. She otherwise wasn't sure how to handle this. Ignoring it was not an option, although she wished it was. The rest of the morning was fraught with thoughts of Austin. She decided she'd call Pastor Martin after lunch. That time couldn't come soon enough, but it finally did.

"Pastor Martin, I need some advice regarding Austin. I think he's in over his head." She explained his meeting with her that morning, but she didn't disclose what Callie had said about how he acted on their walk the night before.

"I see," said Pastor slowly in response. "This is a very bad situation as you already know. It seems he's stopped listening to those who really care about him and instead turning an ear to anger and rebellion."

"I don't know what to do, Pastor."

"It's not for you to do, Sarah Jo – except to pray. You can never go wrong there. No, this is *his* situation, one he should know better about. So, don't seek him out and don't let him in if he comes to your house. If he does end up on your doorstep just reassure him that you're praying for him. In the meantime, I'll try and make contact. If he ignores me, then he's pretty much on his own."

"Thank you, Pastor."

"Just remember, Sarah Jo, that God's love is stronger than anything the enemy can throw into a person's life – including Austin's."

***

It was hard to shake the sense of responsibility Sarah Jo felt about Austin. Still, it was mostly Callie who had been there for him. So why did she herself feel so bound in helping him? As she mulled that over, it occurred to her that Christians were like one big family who looked out for one another. Still, she couldn't afford to go on a guilt trip about him and his problems; she had other things to think about like her studies. There was one thing she could do for him that Pastor had suggested – prayer! Anyone could do that. In fact, the Bible made the point that we should, and even for our enemies which is what Austin made it plain that they were now. *She* didn't feel that way but he had become offended by what she'd said to him before he literally slammed the door in her face. She would pray!

***

"Callie, I need to think about happy things. This serious stuff has really taken a toll on me," said Sarah Jo in a phone call to her friend toward the end of the week.

"So, what do you suggest?"

"Well, it's not too early to go Christmas shopping. I mean stores are already filling up with gift items."

"That's true. Should we go on Saturday?"

"Yes, let's do that, Cal, and let's ask Abby to go with, okay?"

"Sounds like a plan to me. Do you want to call her or should I, SJ?"

"I will. We can make it for about one, okay? We could meet at Woolery's Department Store. That's pretty centrally located."

"Sure. See you then – and there."

Chapter Fifteen

The girls met as planned and once again conversation swirled around what kind of gifts to get for family and friends. The latter meant shopping separately for one another, so each would do that on their own at a separate time. They had gotten gifts for one another for years. Although not expensive, each gift was selected with care for one another and, of course, for Wendy and Laura as well. It was fun. Of course, no shopping trip would be complete without having a snack somewhere and this trip was no exception. It was generally understood that it would take place after the shopping was finished. So now, they sat in a booth at a new place in Pine Moor – The Snack House. The three girls concurred the food was actually very good, but then what could be messed up with snack items?

"This is great," sighed Sarah Jo. "I've been needing this." She took a bite of her Crispy Bar.

"No kidding," agreed Callie. "I've been cramming for semester exams – plus there have been a few other things going on."

"Such as?" inquired Abby.

"Don't ask," said Sarah Jo, a bit too quickly.

"I already did."

"That's true. Well, I thought maybe Callie would've clued you in by now."

"SJ, I don't talk about it if I can help it," said Callie.

"Well, that's true, and I can understand for sure."

"Talk about *what?*" The friends had roused Abby's curiosity.

"It's Austin," said Callie finally. "He's got some problems."

"Don't we all?" asked Abby as she went for another nacho.

"Well yes, but this is different," said Sarah Jo.

"Different *how?*" probed Abby. Callie and Sarah Jo looked at each other.

"Well, he's kind of just morphed back into the old Austin," said Callie. Sarah Jo was glad she had answered. She felt it was more Callie's business than her own.

"*Morphed?*" asked Abby. "You mean he's gone back into that so-called church?"

"No, nothing like that. He's just kind of slipped back into that attitude, though." Callie proceeded to tell Abby what had happened. Sarah Jo added her remarks to clarify as needed.

"What's *wrong* with that guy?"

"Well Abby, it's something called mind control," said Callie. "It's kind of complicated, but in a way it's kind of simple."

"Yeh, but he's been out for a while now," said Abby.

"Doesn't matter. If you're brainwashed, let's say, by an outfit like that you'll probably need to deprogram as it's put. That usually involves counseling. But it can't hurt a thing to be praying for him."

"Wowww..." said Abby softly.

"Yes," said Sarah Jo. "I met with Pastor Martin and that's what he advised." They were about to leave when suddenly Austin appeared at the door. Upon spying the girls, he started to back up, appeared to think better of it, and then entered the small shop. Sarah Jo wondered if he would acknowledge any of them and that was soon answered for her. It appeared Austin made eye contact with Callie but soon went to the counter where he placed his order. Abby, obviously surprised, spoke out boldly to him.

"Hey Austin, are you just going to ignore your friends?" Abby was never one to mince words. Austin turned around as if surprised to see them sitting there.

"Oh, hi," he replied. "I'm in a hurry. Gotta get going."

"Aw, c'mon," she persisted. "Don't tell me you haven't got time for us. There's always time for friends." A pained expression spread across Austin's face. He looked conflicted, then finally relented.

"Oh okay, but just for a couple minutes," he said. He paid for his purchase and came over to where they were sitting.

"Haven't heard from you in a couple days," said Callie. "I wondered if you might be sick or something. I was going to call."

"Well, I've had better days," said Austin. "But I'm okay."

"Have a seat," invited Abby as she moved over in the booth. "We don't bite. Promise." That eased the tension as the girls laughed; even Austin did. He slid into the booth but it was apparent to Sarah Jo that he was more than a little uncomfortable. "So, how have you been doing?" asked Abby.

"Truth? Not the greatest."

"How come?" asked Abby pretending to know nothing about his latest problems. She dipped into her bag of caramel corn. "Want some?" Austin declined.

"Look," he said. "I know you girls know what's going on. You're all friends. I'm sure you talk to each other."

"Yes, but you're our friend too," reminded Sarah Jo.

"What I'm saying is, I'm sure you all know what's going on with me right now." There was a pained expression on his face.

"Please tell us," said Abby, as if totally unaware of what had been going on in Austin's life.

"Well, for one thing it has to do with that game I always had with me. Not everyone likes it, I guess."

"Who's the 'everyone', Austin?" asked Abby.

"It doesn't matter, but people are concerned about it – and *me*."

"How so?" Sarah Jo figured Abby might want to consider a career as an investigative reporter.

"It doesn't matter, but I have to say that Pastor Martin found out and more than hinted that there might be evil forces associated with that game and that I should get rid of it."

"Um – burn it?" reminded Sarah Jo.

"What*ever...*" said Austin impatiently. "Look, I gotta go. I got stuff to do."

"Wait Austin," said Abby, all too quickly. "We're your friends. We want to help."

"How can you guys help?"

"Like this," replied Abby. She reached her hand out to Austin and Callie, and the other two girls joined hands, as did Austin. "Heavenly Father," began Abby. "Austin is dealing with heavy stuff and we need your help. He's our friend and we get that he's in pain. Please heal and protect him." Each of the others contributed to the prayer and when it was Austin's turn he finished it out with an "Amen!" The whole mood at the table had changed.

"Wow! Thanks," said Austin.

"Where *is* that game, by the way, Austin?" asked Sarah Jo.

"Oh, it's at home," answered Austin, brushing off her question.

"I have an idea. Let's take that game and follow through on burning it up. That way no one can ever get hurt by it again," said Sarah Jo.

"Good idea," agreed Callie. Abby nodded.

"I'll call Pastor and ask him if we can do that over at the church. He shouldn't mind. I can't think of a better place. Besides, that cardboard and metal only has as much power as we give it," said Sarah Jo. "I'll call and then email you and let you know what he says and when we can do it. Will sometime on Saturday work for all of you?" They all agreed that day would work the best for everyone.

***

Pastor Martin was concerned that Austin hadn't followed through on the disposing of the game and readily agreed to getting rid of it on Saturday. So when the group had gathered there was no question as to why it was being done. Austin made one remark that showed his reluctance in that he asked if this wasn't like the book burnings that had been held at various times throughout history as a means of controlling information.

"Why, Austin, I'm surprised you'd ask that. If you have any desire to keep this game, you certainly have that right."

"It just seems like we're being superstitious or something..." his words trailed off.

"I wouldn't call it being superstitious, not if you know your Bible," replied Pastor Martin. "Oh, that's right. You used a different type of Bible, didn't you?" The group went outside and around to the back of the church to burn the offending game. There was no need to ask for trouble by burning it inside, Pastor Martin told the small group. Enough damage had been caused by it.

"At least it's not a windy day," commented Abby.

"That's true," agreed Pastor Martin. "First I'd like to just say a short prayer, and Austin, I'd like you to light the match." Pastor produced a box of what Dad called farmer matches, the kind used in farm kitchens to light stoves years ago. "And so, Lord, we ask a blessing and anointing on the one who is burning this game and what it represents. Go ahead, son." Austin struck the match against the box and a flame shot out from it. He touched it to the cardboard and it reluctantly began to burn, a little at first as it caught, then to bright orange and yellow and then fizzled into a darkened ash. Of course, the metal pointer remained, blackened, and Pastor told Austin to just throw it into the small dumpster for the next trash pickup.

"That's funny," declared Austin. "I somehow feel different. I can't explain it, but just *different.*"

"Well, what we're doing here is symbolic in a number of ways," said Pastor Martin. "For one thing, it represents secret sins that we cling to, knowingly or unknowingly, and that applies to all of us. But the game itself has a questionable history. It had to go." Pastor Martin then said a parting blessing on all of them as a good way to end their time together.

***

At dinner, Sarah Jo decided to tell her parents and Mark what happened. That way if Pastor mentioned it to them at church they wouldn't be clueless about the situation.

"So you're saying that game was burned up at Pastor Martin's request?" asked Mom.

"That's about it," answered Sarah Jo. "It wasn't really a request but some rather strong advice."

"Wow – cool!" declared Mark as he helped himself to a drumstick from the plate of fried chicken.

"Well something had to be done," said Sarah Jo. "Austin was really acting different."

"In what way?" asked Dad.

"He just wasn't himself," replied Sarah Jo. "It's like he really had this attitude." She opened up a hot biscuit and slathered the wound with butter.

"What kind of an attitude, Sarah Jo? I mean was he like some monster?"

"Mark! Don't act like a jerk. He's a believer," reminded Sarah Jo. "Christians can be influenced by wrong activities, but it doesn't mean that they're evil. They belong to Jesus."

"Well, if it had that negative an effect on him, then it's a blessing that he's gotten beyond that," said Mom. "Let's change the subject." And they did.

***

Christmas was just around the corner. Sarah Jo had no idea where the school year was going. Before long, she would be graduating from home school. It would be celebrated as a true achievement just as much as with public school graduates. Sarah Jo knew a number of kids from public school since there were some in the church as well as in community activities. She looked forward to graduation with some trepidation, but mainly because it was such a huge step toward her future. It would be very important to choose her steps wisely. She knew she would be attending college, but felt it might be helpful to attend a local two year school to get started. That way she could live at home as well as work part time and help save money toward the rest of her college career.

***

After church about a week before Christmas, a grinning Austin caught up with Sarah Jo and Callie.

"Hey, guess what!" he said breathlessly. "I'm doing better than ever on the court; you know, basketball. In fact, I went to the doctor and he told me that he sees no evidence of an injury."

"That's great!" said Sarah Jo. "Sounds like a healing to me."

"No kidding!" said Callie. "I knew you were playing again but this is great news!"

"Yep, and get this. Coach says I won't be on the sidelines as long as I keep playing like I have lately in practice."

"Boy, Christmas has come early for you."

"It sure has, Sarah Jo, but I think we all know why concerning this sudden turn of events, don't we?"

"I'd say so," said Callie. "Maybe it would be nice to tell Pastor Martin about it."

"That's just what I was about to do." Austin turned on his heel and approached their pastor.

"Wow!" said Callie. "Can you believe it?"

"Yes, yes I can." replied Sarah Jo, smiling. At the moment life seemed good with her friends in the decorated church, so much so that it seemed that nothing could change things but it would. They all were about to get the surprise of their lives. Only a few days later Sarah Jo got the news that Pastor Martin had noticed the Christmas tree was leaning a bit to one side and decided to do something about it. He got on a step ladder and then, just like that, the ladder went down – and so did he. Mom, who'd told the family what had happened said that, thankfully, he'd not broken anything but he was bruised and sore. Sarah Jo mentioned it to Callie over the phone that Wednesday and they both wondered about services on Christmas Eve.

"I don't know if he can handle it," said Sarah Jo. "Mom said he sprained his ankle pretty badly."

"Hey, I think we should see about helping if we can. Let me talk to Austin about it and maybe you can check with Abby."

"That's a great idea, Callie, but how can *we* help? I mean there are some things only a minister can do."

"Well, we can pray about it for starters. After that maybe it would be a good idea to check with Pastor Martin himself."

"That makes sense," said Sarah Jo. "The most he can do is say he doesn't need the help."

"Okay, so I'll call Austin right now. You can text me about Abby's answer if you want later on. I've gotta help Mom with the dishes right now," said Callie.

Abby was "all hands on deck" for helping Pastor Martin. She just needed to know where and when, and yes, she'd pray about it as well. A text from Callie indicated Austin was on board too. Not only that, but Austin wanted to ask Pastor himself just how they could help. To Sarah Jo's way of thinking, this was the turning point for Austin. He was all in on helping their disabled pastor.

***

By Friday, everything was in order. Pastor Martin had a list of chores he normally took care of right before Christmas such as making sure that families in town that were in need had food and gifts for Christmas. He usually made the deliveries himself because it gave him great joy to do so. He could also welcome those people to attend the church as well. Pastor Martin also needed to get gifts and wrap them for the elders, deacons and deaconesses so that was a job the four could do. Friday found the small group doing just that. They put their heads together and decided what to get for each person on the list Pastor had given them, as they sat at one of the tables in the food court at the mall. It would give them the opportunity to brainstorm on gifts and make shopping easier.

"You know," said Austin. "I really should get something for Pastor Martin. He saved my bacon over that wacky board game I had."

"That's a good idea," said Callie, who nodded approvingly.

"But what would you get him?" asked Abby. "He probably has just about everything he needs."

"Not *everything*," said Sarah Jo.

"What do you mean?" asked Austin.

"My mom heard through the ladies group at church that he's always wanted a nice pen and stationery set like for when he writes a note to one of the congregation. He likes that personal touch, I guess."

"How do you know he doesn't already have one by now?" asked Abby as she shifted in her chair.

"Well, Mom said that it's not likely a woman would get it for him, and probably none of the men would think to do it," said Sarah Jo.

"Good point," remarked Austin. "I'll check it out today." He took a long drink from his soda.

"Well, well, well," said one Fern Samuels with her daughter Olivia in tow. "Interesting who you meet at the mall these days. How are you kids doing?"

"Uh, we were just leaving," said Sarah Jo. "We've got a lot to do." The group got up from the table and hurried away.

"Thanks SJ," whispered Callie. "I didn't need that today."

"Hey, don't leave," said Fern Samuels. "I was just trying to be friendly." But it was too late. The group was hurrying off and she was left to stand with her daughter. As the group gathered later after what they deemed a successful shopping expedition, they wondered why Fern Samuels would even approach them. None of them had a desire to see her, let alone talk with her.

"I suppose that's her definition of love – forgive and forget," said Austin. That shocked the rest.

"She's a dangerous person to say the least," said Callie. "She caused you enough trouble for a lifetime, Austin. She can't be trusted."

"I suppose you're right," replied Austin. "That game alone almost cost me my basketball ambitions, not to mention my friendships." He cast a nervous glance in the girls' direction.

"Well, you have nothing to worry about now," said Sarah Jo. "We were kind of looking out for you. As for Fern Samuels, all bets are off."

"Hey," said Abby indignantly, "I don't bet." The group laughed. Leave it to Abby to take things seriously.

***

Christmas was finally upon them. There was Christmas Eve and services which the Foster family was looking forward to. It was an end of the year treat when they could all be together without interruption and focus on all things spiritual and family. The combination of everything – the celebrations, her family, even the light snow on Christmas Eve - caused Sarah Jo to feel an intense sense of thankfulness. She realized how blessed she was to live in a free country, worship where and how she pleased and to speak freely as well.

***

Christmas Day brought a scrumptious meal to the Foster table. This year they decided it would be nice to invite a couple widows from the church to enjoy it with them, Mrs. Swanson and Mrs. Peech. They'd been in the congregation for years and often accompanied each other to various functions. Mrs. Swanson, who Sarah Jo figured to be the elder of the two was tall and thin, whereas Mrs. Peech was a more rounded and shorter individual. She may well have been younger but none of that mattered to Sarah Jo.

"So ladies, shall we get seated? I can tell you that it's smelled mighty good in this kitchen the past couple of days," said Mr. Foster. He pulled out a chair for each and seated them.

"Oh, it smells wonderful in here," exclaimed Mrs. Peech as she sat down at the table.

"Indeed it does," concurred Mrs. Swanson. "Mark, you seem like you might be hungry, am I right?"

"Yes ma'am," Mark nodded enthusiastically. Mrs. Foster approached the table with the roast turkey and set it down in front of her husband.

"Mmmm.... all for me?" he asked, chuckling. Everyone laughed. He wasted no time in wielding the carving knife which resulted in a platter of juicy turkey slices.

"My, my," said Mrs. Peech. "I don't know when I've ever smelled something this good."

"I'm sure you must've been quite a cook yourself, Mrs. Peech, so I imagine you've smelled good food like that many times," said Mrs. Foster.

"Oh, I have made many a Thanksgiving and Christmas meal, dear. Harold – God rest his soul – never complained."

"I can just imagine," replied Mrs. Foster. "Sarah Jo, will you bring the gravy to the table? Oh, and the cranberries too. There, I think we're all set. Will you say grace, dear?" asked Mrs. Foster, nodding in her husband's direction.

"I think I'll let Mrs. Swanson do the honors," he replied. He knew that she was the oldest one there and might be honored by the opportunity.

"Thank you, dear Lord, for your wonderful bounty and these loving friends who've invited us to their table. Please bless those in need and bless this food; in Jesus' name we pray." And they all said, "Amen." During dinner, their two guests told the Fosters stories of their Christmases growing up and that gifts were hard to come by but ever so much appreciated.

"I remember the year we had so much snow that we were actually snowed in. In those days it wasn't uncommon for snow banks, after the snow plow finally came through, to be almost as high as the power poles along the main roads. Side roads didn't get plowed until later," said Mrs. Peech.

"How did you get food?" asked Mark.

"That was the least of our worries, son. We put up most of our own food and we still had milk from our cows," she explained. "The problem might've been if we'd needed to see the doctor. We'd have to find a way to get there but, thankfully, we never had that kind of an emergency." Sarah Jo couldn't imagine living like that. She was glad she lived in modern times.

"I do remember that year, Helen," said Mrs. Swanson. "It snowed and snowed, then turned bitter cold. Oh my, was it cold!"

"Shall we have dessert?" asked Mrs. Foster, as she got up from the table. "Sarah Jo and Mark, would you clear the table?"

"Mom, are you going to use the French press for coffee that Mark and I got you?"

"Yes, Sarah Jo, plus the beans that your father got to go with it as well. Go get that coffee grinder I picked up at a tag sale last summer, please."

"Yes, Mom," said Sarah Jo, then hurried off to the cabinet to look.

"That dessert and coffee were almost as good as the dinner," remarked Mrs. Peech. "I don't know when I've had coffee this good."

"Would you like more?" asked Mrs. Foster. Mrs. Peech shook her head no while gesturing away from her coffee cup with her palm. Her mouth was now full with her last bite of pumpkin pie.

"I do believe I will, dear," said Mr. Foster, "and another piece of your pie too. Those pumpkins we grew really were good this year."

"Me too!" chimed in Mark, "..uh, just pie, please."

The afternoon ended on a high note. The ladies left for home while it was yet light out and not snowing, although it was in the forecast for that evening.

Chapter Sixteen

Morning found the town of Pine Moor snowed in. Much snow had been predicted, but a lot more had fallen. Not only that, but the wind was starting to blow it around. That morning at breakfast Mom and Dad were discussing the situation.

"Do you *have* to go into work, dear?" asked Mom.

"I really can't get out of it," replied Dad. "This is an important client and it's a rush situation. I'll take the four wheel drive. I'll be okay."

"Isn't that dangerous, Dad?" asked Sarah Jo.

"Not unless the other guy doesn't have four wheel drive," chuckled Dad who was trying to make light of it for the sake of his family. "They'll probably have the roads plowed by the time I head for home."

"I hate to ask this of you, but if you remember, will you pick up some milk on your way home? We're getting low," suggested Mom.

"Sure thing, hon." Then Dad was off. Sarah Jo watched as he skillfully backed down the driveway and on to the main road and made his way to work. It was only a few miles, but the road would be horrific. That part was guaranteed.

"Did he make it out okay?" asked Mom as she joined Sarah Jo at the window.

"He's out of sight now," replied Sarah Jo. "If it snows any more, though, it's not going to be good."

"I should say not!" declared her mother. Mark bounded down the stairs.

"What did I miss?"

"Well, Dad for one. He left for work in spite of the snow," said Sarah

Jo. "I think I'm going to get on the computer and check out my English Lit so I'll be ready for my midterms."

"I'm glad I still go to regular school for now. At least I get to be on my basketball team," said Mark.

"You still could even if you were home schooled, at least I think so. But unless you plan to make a career of basketball, I'd say academics come first."

"Aw sis, you always have to spoil it for me, don't you?"

"No, cuz I don't have the last word. But regardless, you always have the home school group to play basketball with. So you'll never have to give it up."

***

That afternoon Sarah Jo got a surprise call from Wendy in Addison. Although Addison was a few hours away it sounded as though they'd gotten a worse snow storm than Pine Moor had.

"Oh my gosh, Sarah Jo. You wouldn't believe the snow we've got here!" exclaimed Wendy.

"Well, I would if you'd take your phone and get me some pics."

"I'm not going out in this stuff, but I'll take some from the front door," returned Wendy obligingly.

"My dad was brave. He went to work today," said Sarah Jo.

"No! Really?"

"Yep. Nothing scares my dad, or if it does, he doesn't show it."

"Did you have a good Christmas?" asked Wendy in a sudden change of subject.

"It was really nice, but then, what could be bad about Christmas?"

"How's Austin doing?"

"Ever since we burned that horrible board game – if you want to call it that – he's been doing well. He's even healed up enough to play basketball. I'm glad he got to the point of seeing how evil that board game was, Wendy."

"How's Callie doing? I'll bet she's much happier without that game around."

"No kidding! She's a *lot* happier."

"Well, I'm glad to hear that. I pray for you guys every day. For awhile I was getting really worried. It's like all these bad things kept happening to Austin."

"I know," said Sarah Jo. "It was pretty creepy."

"Well, I s'pose I'd better get going. It's not like I'm going anywhere in this stuff, but Mom has some things she wants me to do." The girls said their goodbyes and each got on with their day. Sarah Jo was glad she had Wendy for a friend.

***

The new year brought some exciting prospects Sarah Jo's way. She knew she wanted to go to the local college although it would provide only a two year course of studies. She'd hoped to save money by living at home, plus she wasn't in a great hurry to leave the family. That would come soon enough. Callie had told her of her own plans to become a counselor in light of her experiences with Future Life Fellowship where she'd met Austin – and Fern Samuels. She told Sarah Jo how she felt sorry for her daughter Olivia who through no choice of her own would be, for all intents and purposes, forced to follow their legalistic rules. Perhaps at some future time when Olivia was older she'd come to know the Lord in a special way and special relationship. Or perhaps someone would teach her, maybe even Callie.

***

Sarah Jo was surprised when a couple of nights later she heard from Luke Holman with whom she double dated with Callie and Austin at Homecoming. She hardly recognized his voice even though it was only a few months earlier that they went as a foursome to the Homecoming dance.

"So, how have you been?" asked Luke.

"I've been doing well. I mean, how could I not when it comes to Christmas?"

"Was Santa good to you?" he joked.

"Well, Santa or some other good people in my life. We sure have had a dumpload of snow from Mother Nature, haven't we?"

"No kidding. It's been a mess. Say, Sarah Jo, I was just wondering if you might want to go out sometime – I mean sometime when there isn't a ton of snow on the ground."

"What did you have in mind?"

"Oh, maybe a show or maybe bowling or something. Do you bowl?" Sarah Jo laughed.

"If you want to call it that."

"Well, call it what you will, we could do that or something else."

"Would this be just the two of us or a foursome like last time?"

"Hey, I have no problem if Callie and Austin want to join us – just as long as that board game doesn't come along."

"It's not going anywhere anymore," assured Sarah Jo.

"So, is that a yes?"

"Yes – yes it is. I'll check with Callie and see if she and Austin want to go," said Sarah Jo.

"Who was that, honey?" asked Mom as she walked by her open bedroom door. She had clean folded towels in her hands for the linen closet.

"Oh, it was just Luke Holman – remember him? He took me to the Homecoming dance."

"Of course I remember him, dear. Very nice young man."

"Yes, he was – even in spite of all that happened that night," said Sarah Jo. Mom just shook her head. It turned out that Callie and Austin were enthusiastic about a double date – a term that Sarah Jo hesitated using. She felt it was too much to describe the relationship she and Luke had, which was essentially a friendship. It did describe, though, the fact that they'd all be going together.

***

"Guys, wait up!" yelled Callie as the group made their way to the door at Bodie's Bowling Center. Callie was wearing dress boots instead of practical snow boots like Sarah Jo had chosen. She'd gotten them for Christmas and she was going to make good use of them this winter. She didn't know when Callie had gotten the boots she was wearing but they were totally impractical at this time of year – and with this much snow.

"Need some help, Cal?" asked Austin, chuckling. "I can carry you to the door if you like."

"No, it's just going to take me a little longer is all." They entered the building and the sound of strikes reverberated, along with music. They got their shoes and prepared for a night of fun. All but Sarah Jo had bowled before. Actually, she tried it once with the family in Addison but she couldn't see the fun in it. But she did her best with the other three and came through with beginners luck. That was probably because Wendy had helped her and gave her tips along the way. Her friend Laura in Addison was good too. She just guessed that she herself wasn't that coordinated.

About halfway through their evening, who shows up but Fern Samuels? She was accompanied by a group of teens that Sarah Jo guessed was from her so-called church. What luck! Or *was* it luck? She was concerned about how Austin or even Callie might handle things.

"Sarah Jo!" called Callie in a hoarse whisper. "Check out who's here."

"Yeah, I noticed before. Lucky us!" Mrs. Samuels had already side-lined Austin and engaged him in conversation. Fern Samuels didn't look too pleased.

"We were here first," said Callie in a mock complaining tone of voice. As if on cue, Austin smiled and said "You too" to the older woman and made his way back to their group.

"Wow, you're brave!" remarked Callie as she picked up her bowling ball and cupped it underneath with her other hand.

"How so?" asked Austin. Callie assumed her stance, stepped forward, let the ball go and followed through. She knocked down all but two pins.

"Just that it would be hard to see her again after all she's done to you." Callie knocked down the remaining pins.

"Callie you, better than anyone, should know that Jesus taught us to love our enemies. There's a reason for that."

"True, she was not very kind to me either and I've forgiven her, but I don't trust her at all." They sat down.

"Well, I don't think the Bible says we have to trust someone who has hurt us," said Sarah Jo. "I think forgiveness is the main thing."

"You know I believe in God and all," said Luke, "but I won't go out of my way to make myself available to be hurt by someone." Sarah Jo glanced in Fern Samuels' direction and noticed how she was making broad, sweeping gestures to the group of teens with her. She certainly wasn't explaining bowling technique, but probably religious ideas from her cult organization. The kids, she noticed, were sitting quietly looking down with their hands, folded. They probably were being lectured on how to act. How much fun was *that?* she wondered. On the way home, Austin told the group what Mrs. Samuels had said.

"I didn't want to say anything in public about our conversation, but I don't see a problem in telling you now. Mrs. Samuels asked how I was doing and if I was happy and that I was sorely missed, as she put it, by everyone at Future Life Fellowship."

"How did you answer her?" asked Callie.

"I told her that things were going okay. She did ask one question that I wasn't sure how to answer. She asked if I was still enjoying that board game *Spin and Win – or Not!*"

"What did you say?" asked Sarah Jo and Callie at the same time.

"I just told her I didn't have it any more, which is true."

"What happened to it?" asked Luke, as he slowed down to a stop at the railroad tracks.

"It's kind of a long story," said Callie, "but I'll tell you if you really want to know. He did, so she explained. There were no blanks to be filled in by the time she got finished.

"I can't believe it!" Luke declared incredulously.

"You have to," said Austin. "Cuz it's the truth."

"You mean that woman in there used to own it?"

"Yep," said Austin, "until she put it in the silent auction that our church put on for its members."

"Did she have bad luck or karma when *she* owned it?" asked Luke.

"We don't usually refer to it as either luck *or* karma," volunteered Callie. "We usually bring bad stuff upon ourselves with a little help from the enemy."

"Oh..." said Luke, his voice trailing off.

"Hey, maybe you'd like to come to our church sometime," said Sarah Jo. "You might find it interesting."

"I'd be okay with that."

"Good! Then it's settled. Maybe this Sunday... okay?" asked Callie.

"Uh, sure," replied Luke.

"Well, this is my stop," said Callie. "Thanks for the ride." She waved as she walked to her door.

"You next, Austin," said Luke. Austin got out at the end of his driveway.

"I'd take you up to your door, but I don't want to get stuck in this snow."

"That's okay, Luke. The driveway needs to be plowed again, so I can't blame you. See you at practice."

"So, now I'll get you home, Sarah Jo. I hope you had at least *some* fun bowling, even if it isn't your strong suit as you put it."

"I did have fun, Luke. It's always nice to get out and try things you haven't done for awhile – even things you don't remember having been good at the first time around." They chuckled.

✳✳✳

That Sunday found the four friends together once again. They decided they'd all sit together at church. That way Luke wouldn't have to sit alone, although by now he'd been introduced to a number of people in the congregation including Pastor Martin and his wife.

"Just so you know, Luke, as a visitor here you're not obligated to do what the rest of us do whether it be standing, singing or whatever," said Sarah Jo.

"No problem," answered Luke. "I don't necessarily like standing *out* either." To Sarah Jo's way of thinking, the service went really well. Pastor spoke about "our light trials" such as the weather, compared to what the apostle Paul went through in his travels as he brought the grace gospel to people is Asia Minor and environs.

***

At lunch, which usually was a lighter meal for the Fosters, Sarah Jo told her family about Luke enjoying the service and that he found Pastor Martin's sermon interesting.

"I'm glad he did," said Mom. "That man has a lot of wisdom."

"Who?" asked Mark, "Luke or Pastor Martin?"

"Who do you think?" asked Dad.

"Well, maybe both of them. I only know Pastor Martin," replied Mark as he gulped down the remainder of his milk.

"You're silly!" said Sarah Jo. "You know good and well that Mom was talking about Pastor."

"You never know. Luke might become a pastor too." He used his sleeve to wipe off his milk mustache.

"Well, I sure hope *you* don't unless you lose that nasty habit. Why didn't you use your napkin? It's not there just for looks."

"Nobody asked you, Sarah Jo," retorted Mark. "May I be excused?"

"Yes – after you apologize to your sister," said Dad.

"Sorry," Mark jumped up from the table.

***

That evening Luke called. Sarah Jo wondered why he might be calling since she'd just seen him earlier that day.

"Hey Sarah Jo, I was just wondering if you might want to go out Friday night."

"What did you have in mind?"

"I thought we could go sledding on Olsen's Hill. Maybe Austin and Callie would want to go too."

"That could be fun, especially if there's no blizzard or something." They chuckled. "You and Austin don't have a game that night?"

"No, that would be the following week."

"I'll check with Callie and see if she has anything going on that night."

"Great. I'll call Austin and then call you to see if it's a go." The other two were enthusiastic about the plans too. They all would be sledding that Friday night. Since Sarah Jo had taken on temporary work before the holidays at a quaint little store called the Holiday Shop she had hours during the week, but Mrs. Carroll had said she could handle things herself now so Sarah Jo didn't need to go in on Saturday. It got very busy just between Thanksgiving and Christmas, but now it had quieted down.

***

That Friday the foursome decided to go to Connie's Cocoa Cottage for some hot chocolate before heading over to Olsen's Hill. Everyone in the group was in high spirits partly because the weather was just right – not too cold out – as well as the fact that they all got along really well. Their night ended with a mix of laughing and exhaustion after making multiple treks up the hill and then enjoying the rewards going down.

"I think you have the right idea with that Mini 'boggan," said Austin to Sarah Jo.

"Well, at least it has room for a passenger," came her reply as she transported the small and lightweight plastic toboggan to Luke's parents' SUV.

"Me? I'll take snowboarding any day," said Luke.

"Me too," agreed Callie. "The only problem is I'd probably be sitting in the snow most of the time. You really have to have good balance." She pulled her mother's good "broke in" sled from years ago. It could really fly down the hills. Her dad had even made a removable back and sides so that as a child Callie could be placed in it and pulled by him in newly fallen snow when her parents went for a walk.

"So, to your house first, Sarah Jo?"

"I think so, Luke. All this fresh air has made me tired."

"Okay then. Off we go to the Foster residence. Where are those jingle bells when you need them?"

Chapter Seventeen

Sarah Jo had taken advantage of the same Christmas break that the kids at public school had, but now it was time to get "back in the harness," as Dad would say. In her terms, it was time to hit the books. She felt renewed from her break from her studies so she was anxious to face the new semester vigorously. It seemed strange to be so close to being out on her own, although she planned to live with Mom and Dad yet while she attended the local college. That would be a new experience since she was used to being schooled at home, but she looked forward to the challenge of being in an actual brick and mortar school. The campus wasn't that far away, but winter travel might be challenging. She would trust God to get her back and forth safely. That evening Callie called.

"You know, Sarah Jo, I don't know if Fern Samuels will ever be out of my life."

"What do you mean?"

"She called Austin on Sunday night and guess what she did – she invited him over for dinner."

"*What?*"

"Yep, it's true, and you know what else? She invited me along as well."

"You aren't going, Cal, are you?"

"I wasn't going to; neither was Austin, but then she said something that made Austin change his mind."

"What's that?" asked Sarah Jo.

"She told Austin that if what he believes is so great, he shouldn't mind showing it toward others."

"She was referring to being a Christian, I take it."

"You got it, SJ. I had to admit I could see her point. So Austin accepted the invite and so did I."

"Really?" exclaimed Sarah Jo incredulously.

"Yep. Who knows how we are called to witness?"

"That's true, but aren't you scared?"

"Scared of what? What is she going to do with us, put us down in her basement after we keel over from poisoned food?" Callie chuckled.

"Maybe you should bring a taster along, right?" The girls both giggled over the prospect.

"Nahhh, I'll just let her take the first bite."

"When are you going?" asked Sarah Jo.

"It's set up for Friday night."

"Austin doesn't have a game?"

"No, it's on Saturday afternoon. It's a home game so I'll probably go."

"If you survive the dinner, that is. Sorry, I apologize."

"Well, she's given me no reason to trust her, but God is a God of second chances, so I suppose I should be willing to give her another chance also," said Callie.

"I know, and to overcome evil with good, right?"

"Right! Or at least try to anyway."

***

The following Saturday it didn't take long to see how the dinner went. Callie was quick to call Sarah Jo and give her the full report.

"So, did you have a good time?" asked Sarah Jo.

"You wouldn't believe it!"

"That good, huh?"

"Good? I might describe it, but not necessarily *that* way," said Callie.

"Out with it, girl!" Sarah Jo wondered what could have happened that would cause Callie to respond that way to her initial question.

"First of all, it was a dinner if you want to call it that – a couple salads, 'health bread' that was like sandpaper, and stuffed baked pumpkin with some sort of vegetable grain in the stuffing."

"Really? Was it good?"

"Well, only if you like a vegetarian meal. I had a hard time with that stuffing."

"Hmmm..."

"But here's the kicker. After dinner, people began to arrive – all from her church, or so she said. They were there for the Bible study."

"*What??*"

"Yep – believe it or not!"

"Do I have a choice?" asked Sarah Jo.

"Not really, cuz that's the way it happened."

"What did you do?"

"Well, as they say, we knocked 'em dead!" proclaimed Callie.

"What – *really?*"

"Yep! I think we really shocked 'em."

"Give me an example."

"Well, okay. During their Bible study one woman who Austin knew said he'd done wrong by not doing whatever was necessary to get back in their group. She really kinda let him have it for that."

"So what did Austin say?"

"He said that God is not about a group and that He is to be worshiped in spirit and in truth. That's not to say that people can't or shouldn't belong to a church, just that God is a Spirit and must be worshiped in spirit and truth."

"Bet they didn't like hearing that," said Sarah Jo.

"No kidding! They looked at him like he came from outer space or something."

"Wow! You two were really brave in accepting that invitation. I'll bet Fern Samuels wished she'd never invited you guys over."

"Maybe so, SJ. I mean she really should have told us it was a Bible study more than a dinner. I don't like the idea of fighting for my beliefs, but I don't want people insisting that lies are the truth, and deceiving others."

"Can't blame you. Well, I'd better get going. Thanks for sharing with me, Callie. I'll pray that those people will come to see the light someday – hopefully sooner rather than later."

"Kinda hard to do that when they don't even have the right Christ. The one they look to is an imaginary being from a false version of a book in the Bible," said Callie.

"All the more reason to pray, Cal, right?"

***

The next day was bitterly cold and even though Sarah Jo had planned to take a nice long walk, that plan was scuttled. She had some thinking to do and she always did it better when walking. The fresh air cleared her head and the briskness of outdoors helped with the thinking process. Not so today. Instead, she would hunker down and delve into her studies once again. She wanted to make the most of her senior year since what she did would be on the record. Perhaps a project could enhance that record. Maybe she could come up with something that would have a meaningful impact this final year of high school. That was part of what she'd wanted to think about during her postponed walk. The other subject was totally different, but nevertheless worth thinking about as well. She needed to think about Luke and how he fit into her life. She didn't want to give the wrong impression that he was anything more than a friend, but maybe he thought she was. Still, it wasn't like how things were between Callie and Austin. They took their relationship seriously but Sarah Jo wasn't even sure what *that* was. Maybe even Callie didn't know, but she and Austin dated quite frequently. Finally, Sarah Jo came to a conclusion on the matter, the one she least looked forward to. She would need to speak to Luke about the situation before there was a misunderstanding or hurt feelings. It might as well be in person. She needed for them to see one another's facial expressions to get a good read on things.

A text to Luke the next day provided the opportunity Sarah Jo was looking for. Luke casually mentioned getting together on Saturday afternoon for skating at a pond near Connie's Cocoa Cottage. It so happened that Connie's husband had built that pond close enough to the Cocoa Cottage that it would draw skaters in. Skaters would also have it as a warming house nearby; it was a very popular spot in the winter. Luke was going to be picking her up and it would be just the two of them since Sarah Jo needed some privacy to discuss what she needed to with him. Otherwise the double dating, if one could call it that, usually included Callie and Austin.

They sat in the booth closest to the fireplace as they sipped their hot cocoa. Sarah Jo hated to spoil the moment; one that seemed to belong on a magazine cover.

"So Sarah Jo, are you ready for what the future holds after this last year of high school?" That caught her completely off guard. She thought she was in charge of this discussion.

"Uhh, well I'm trying to think ahead, yes," This could be to her advantage. "How about you?" She took a sip of cocoa which was plenty hot.

"I am as well. Of course, I'd like a future which includes basketball so college is really important to me. I'll be going to State in the fall."

"Good for you!" said Sarah Jo approvingly. "That's where I plan to attend in a couple years. For now it will be right here in town."

"Hey, part of the same system; later on to State. Great. My first year there I'm really going to have to buckle down. It'll be kinda hard since I want to focus on basketball as well."

"I'm sure you'll do well, Luke. I'm not sure that I could give up family and friends and, of course, my church to attend school. I mean I'll have to anyway in a couple of years but not right out of the starting gate."

"Is that what you think I'll be doing – heading out on a race?" He chuckled.

"It's just a figure of speech; you know what I mean."

"True, and I can understand what you mean by leaving family and friends, but *church?* Churches are a dime a dozen. You can find them anywhere."

"Not all churches are created equal, Luke. You might want to talk to Austin about that."

"Why? I really don't know him that well. He only joined the team a year or so ago. That's where I met him. Nice guy."

"Well, he'll tell you a story you won't believe." I wouldn't either except that Callie saw it with her own eyes."

"*What* are you talking about?"

"Just ask Austin if all churches are created equal, so to speak."

"Sarah Jo, what is all this stuff about God and churches?"

"Hey Luke, you're the one that asked. After you hear Austin's story I'll be more than happy to fill you in about God and churches, as you put it."

"You're on!" said Luke enthusiastically as if it were a challenge. Sarah Jo knew now that their relationship wasn't about anything serious – at least not between the two of *them*, which was a relief. It looked as though God had given her an "assignment." She gladly accepted.

***

Several weeks later Sarah Jo was surprised to get a phone call from Luke. She was eating the last of her sandwich for lunch when her phone played an excerpt from a favorite song she'd chosen as her ringtone. She'd selected an upbeat song from *Joyrush;* and hoped that song heralded some good news.

"Hey Sarah Jo, have you got a few minutes?" Luke sounded out of breath.

"Sure. Actually more than a few. I'm ahead on my work here. What's up?" She'd chosen the project she was considering as an enhancement to her studies – one that would land her some extra credit.

"We had practice yesterday and afterward I talked with Austin as you had suggested I do."

"And?"

"Well, I have to say I'm having a hard time believing what he told me. We talked after practice so we had enough time to talk. He seemed willing enough to tell me about stuff that went on in his life while he was in that church outfit. I just couldn't believe the part about his reason for not signing up for basketball. I mean like not being allowed to wear our uniforms – *really?*"

"Well, it's the truth, believe it or not."

"What a waste of talent all that time before. The guy plays like a pro."

"Yes, and that's why God put him there; at least that's what I believe."

"Boy, Sarah Jo, you talk like you *know* God, like He's a friend."

"He's the best friend *you'll* ever have, Luke."

"Okay, so that's why I called you. Can we meet somewhere and talk about God more? It doesn't have to be today."

"Well, it can be today, if you like. I've got some time this afternoon."

"Okay. How about if I swing by and we hit a coffee shop?"

"Sure. Would three o'clock work for you?"

"Yeh, that'll work fine. See you then." God was providing some serious confirmation on what she wanted to know about her and Luke's relationship. Even though this was not considered a "date" date, she wore her new leggings and tartan plaid sweater; it looked nice and, more importantly, the combo was warm. Luke was punctual as usual. They decided that a newer coffee shop in town, *Hole In The Wall,* would be a nice place to try. They got their coffee and found a place to sit that was in a corner flanked by large planters; she didn't want Luke to be distracted by customers seated in close proximity.

"Wow! This is some coffee shop," declared Luke. "If we ever come back here, I guess this will be *our* table." Sarah Jo laughed.

"Well, it'll be *somebody's* table, I guess." She didn't want to encourage the *our* part of things, especially when there were many more impor-tant things to think about. She decided to launch the discussion first thing. "So Luke, just what *do* you know about God?"

"Hey, you don't waste any time, do you? Well, our family didn't prioritize church or anything. We *did* go, but mainly cuz that was the thing you were sposed to do then."

"What's changed? People probably need it more than ever now." Luke, looking uncomfortable, shifted in his chair.

"Well uh, you don't know my family."

"That's right. I don't. But it's a place to start."

"Well, for starters, my dad opens the hardware store on Sundays."

"Yes, but that's in the afternoon, right?" asked Sarah Jo. "His Sunday mornings are free, aren't they?"

"True, but he usually goes in early to get things ready and to open."

"Hmmm... he couldn't have someone else open, like a trusted employee?" Luke shifted again and was beginning to look a bit uncomfortable.

"I've never talked to him about it. He'd probably ask me to open."

"Oh sorry, Luke. I didn't mean to tell you how he should run his business. I'm just giving an example of what could be done."

"When you own a business it's different. When it comes to your time, it's not your own. It belongs to your customers."

"I see your point. Anyway, you could come to church if you wanted to. I'd be there and so would Austin and Callie."

"I think that would work out okay. Dad doesn't need me to help on Sundays, but I do work there some Saturdays and after school when I don't have practice."

"How's that going for you, Luke? Practice, I mean."

"It's going well, Sarah Jo, thanks."

"My brother Mark is really interested in basketball. Dad put up a hoop on the garage to use for practice. 'Course it doesn't do much good in the dead of winter." They both laughed. An hour later they said their goodbyes and concluded that Luke would go to her church and learn about God for himself. Sarah Jo knew that Luke would get a good education spiritually over a relatively short time, just by attending. Beyond that, she herself would fill in the blanks on the rest. As long as Luke was receptive, Sarah Jo wanted to make sure she did her part.

Still, she didn't want to seem pushy. That would never do on such an important topic.

Chapter Eighteen

The winter plodded on, but it was fun and exciting for Sarah Jo to watch Luke's spiritual progress. Even Callie noticed how much he'd grown spiritually.

"You know, Sarah Jo, I hardly remember the old Luke," she said one afternoon at Connie's Cocoa Cottage. "He not only talks the talk; he walks the walk."

"I know. Isn't that great? He's got a bright future the way things are going."

"One that includes you? I mean you guys are pretty friendly."

"Hey, don't read things into what might not be there, Cal."

"I won't once I'm sure that nothing *is* there," she giggled.

"Not to bring up a sore subject, but have you seen Fern Samuels around town – with or without her daughter?

"No; why would you ask, Sarah Jo?" Callie took a sip of cocoa, her eyes peering over the edge of the cup.

"Oh, no reason in particular, well, maybe except for getting even for you asking about Luke and me." She winked and chuckled.

"Sarah Jo, you're making that up."

"Yes, I am," she agreed. "I think I'll get a refill on that cocoa. Do you want some more?" Callie drank the rest of hers and nodded. Before Sarah Jo could go to the counter, Connie was on her way with a carafe of hot cocoa and a bowl of mini marshmallows.

"I guess I read your minds," said Connie matter-of-factly. "Or maybe it was that I saw you drink down the last of what you had.

"Either way, it brought the cocoa here," chuckled Sarah Jo. Connie served the hot chocolate and left the marshmallows on the table in their bowl, and left.

"Actually, I did see Fern at the library the other day," said Callie. "She asked me about Austin."

"Really?"

"Yes, really.

"What did you tell her?" Sarah Jo took a few mini marshmallows and dropped them into her steaming cocoa.

"I didn't know what to say because I knew she was probably fishing for information."

"So...."

"So I just said I guessed he was doing okay. I tried to keep it simple."

"Did that satisfy her?"

"What do *you* think? Of course not," said Callie. "She was probing. She asked if he was happy with his life and -"

"What? You're kidding!"

"No – I'm not."

"And how did you answer her?"

"The best way I knew how. I told her he was very happy which, to my knowledge, he is."

"Good for you, Cal. That was quick thinking. At least she'll know there's happiness to be found outside of their outfit."

"Yes, but get this. She didn't stop there. She asked what that was attributed to and I couldn't resist answering that question."

"What did you say?" asked Sarah Jo, as she carefully took a sip of her hot cocoa.

"I told her, 'Jesus Christ.'"

"Way to go, Cal. Bet that stopped her in her tracks."

"Or led her to more questions."

"Did she ask something else?"

"Yes, yes she did," answered Callie emphatically. "She asked me if I realized that if I was interfering with God's plan for Austin that I could be in grave danger."

"*What?*"

"That's what she said. She said, 'Just remember. You'll have to give account for that interference.'"

"Callie, that's crazy talk! You haven't done anything wrong."

"I know, SJ, but apparently in her wacky world she thinks I have."

"Well, it doesn't matter what she thinks – she's not God!"

"Ssshhhh.... People will think we're, well... I guess they'll think we're Christians. Come to think of it, that's what I'd like them to think."

"Exactly! This is what sets us apart. We use God's name for something other than to take it in vain," said Sarah Jo.

"So, what do I do if I run into her again? I'm not afraid of her, but I just don't want confrontation."

"Haven't you come across answers for something like that in your cult research, Cal?"

"Well, not specifically, but people like that are argumentative; they sow seeds of discord, so to speak."

"Hmmm... you can't have an argument if it's just one person arguing though," said Sarah Jo.

"That's true," agreed Callie. "You know, I have to resolve this one way or the other. I can't have her dogging me the rest of my life." Connie bustled over to where they were sitting.

"I don't mean to interrupt but you two looked like you needed some more cocoa. Just say the word," said the kindly Connie. Sarah Jo and Callie both thanked her for one last cup of cocoa. They'd need it when they got back out into the cold.

"Hey Connie, you see a lot of people in here so you probably have dealt with all kinds," said Callie.

"Oh, I sure do. I've seen all kinds. Why?"

"Well, just that among all the non-troublemakers, aren't there always a few that can make life difficult?" asked Sarah Jo. She gingerly took a sip from the thick cup of hot cocoa.

"Oh, you better believe it. Why? Are you girls having trouble with someone in particular?"

"Sort of," replied Callie. Connie looked around to make sure no one was listening. No one was because no one else was there.

"What kind of trouble?" asked Connie. "Is it someone I know?"

"It's not *big* trouble," said Callie. "Just sort of like a dog nipping at your heels." Connie laughed.

"Oh, you mean an ankle-biter, huh?"

"Pretty much," said Sarah Jo.

"Yes," concurred Callie, "a real nuisance."

"Well, if I knew who it was I could maybe be of help," said Connie helpfully.

"I don't know if we should say," said Sarah Jo hesitantly.

"That's up to you, but I do know a lot of people," added Connie.

"If we told you, would you keep it to yourself?" asked Callie.

"Do birds fly?" asked Connie in an attempt to lighten things up.

"Some do, but some don't," said Callie, chuckling.

"Tell you what," said Connie. "If I spill the beans on this, I'll give you two cocoas on the house for the rest of the winter, but don't forget to bring your money when you come here, because you're going to need it. I won't be telling *anyone* what you tell me." The girls looked at one another and nodded.

"Okay," they said in unison. Callie began with a bit of history on Fern Samuels. She spoke of her "odd church" and how she came to know Fern.

"Oh, you mean that building that's not a church. Isn't that where they meet?" asked Connie.

"Yes, they don't meet in actual churches," replied Callie.

"Well, I suppose it saves money as far as maintenance and upkeep." commented Connie.

"But anyway, this Fern seems to pop up from time to time at places I just happen to be. It's like she's stalking me, but yet, usually she's quite friendly. Sometimes she has her daughter Olivia with her."

"Yes," added Sarah Jo. "And sometimes when we come to your place here with this tall guy, that's Austin. He used to attend her church, but he quit it a while back."

"Yes," Callie followed through. "And that bugs her like crazy." Connie looked confused.

"Why would anyone go bonkers if someone left the church they both were attending?"

"She's quite the control freak," said Callie, "if you hadn't already guessed that."

"Hmmm," said Connie. "I *do* know of a woman who's come in here a couple times with her young daughter. I've never seen her here with anyone else."

"That could be her, Connie. Does she act weird?" asked Callie who took a sip of the steaming cocoa.

"Weird?" asked Connie. "I'm not sure what you mean by that. She did complain though once and made quite a scene."

"Really?" asked Sarah Jo. "A scene over what?"

"Oh, she complained that the hot cocoa had burned her little girl's lips. Of course the little girl was crying all the while. I brought a glass of cold milk for her to drink and soothe her lips."

"Then what happened?" asked Sarah Jo.

"I had to point out to her the sign above the counter as well as the note on the menus that caution that the cocoa is very hot. She just got up and whisked her little girl out the door. She had quite the scowl on her face – the mother, not the daughter who was still crying."

"That sounds like her," said Callie. "But then I guess that could fit the description of a number of women."

"Wait a minute," said Connie. "I do recall something that might identify her. She was carrying a sort of Bible. She set it down when she paid for her order. It said Holy Bible on the front, but underneath the title it said Alvin Barton Translation. I remember it because at the time I don't recall ever hearing that name of a translation."

"We've got the right person then, Connie," confirmed Callie. "It's her."

"So, what does this mean for you?" asked Connie. A customer entered the Cottage and Connie excused herself.

"That's a good question," said Sarah Jo, "but what is the answer?"

"I don't know, but I *do* know I don't want to go around looking for trouble," replied Callie.

Connie bustled back to their table almost as quickly as she had gone.

"I know what *I'd* do," said Connie. "I'd document these supposed chance encounters right down to the minute. The only thing is, that they've already taken place. I'd see if it happens again and if it does, I'd talk to my pastor if I were you."

"Well, if she thinks that in some universe I'm going to try and influence Austin, she's got another thing coming – like a slice of truth," said Callie. "I mean if you were sitting at a banquet table, why would you go out back and root through the garbage cans. Oops!" Callie looked like she said something unexpectedly and just realized it.

"Oops what?" said Connie.

"Well, I just realized that what I said was kind of insulting to her beliefs," confessed Callie.

"Hey, it's just between us. Yes, she's allowed to believe what she wants, just not to cram those beliefs down someone else's throat," said Sarah Jo.

"Well, Austin can think for himself and somewhere between his leaving that fellowship and now, he's given himself permission to think for himself," said Callie.

"Well said!" declared Sarah Jo.

"That must be some outfit!" said Connie. "In most churches you don't need permission to attend and be approved."

"Trust me, Connie," said Callie, "this is not your average church."

Chapter Nineteen

It was a great surprise to Callie, who told Sarah Jo, that Fern Samuels had not bothered her even once since that conversation at Connie's Cocoa Cottage and Sarah Jo's and Callie's confidential conversation with Connie herself. Winter had pretty much run its course and now the girls were contemplating what to wear to the Spring Formal. Home schooled students were invited to participate which made for harmonious relations between the two groups, the home schooled and the public school students. Anything that could bring the community together was considered a favorable outcome in Pine Moor.

"So, what are you going to wear?" asked Callie.

"I'm not sure; nothing like some of the girls wear. I'd be uncomfortable for one thing, plus I'd probably freeze."

"I know what you mean," said Callie, giggling. "Guys have it great. They can wear a suit or a tux and be fine."

"Maybe, but I wouldn't envy them on a hot and humid day."

"True, but most of the school year takes place in the winter and spring," replied Callie.

"Hey, changing the subject a bit, have you heard from the Addison girls?"

"I did. I heard from Wendy the other day. I guess I forgot to tell you," said Callie.

"What's new with them?"

"Pretty much the usual stuff. Wendy said she really missed us. She said Laura did too."

"We'll have to get together as soon as the weather turns nicer," said Sarah Jo. "We'll all be busy this summer."

"A get together *without* that stupid game of Austin's, right?"

"That's for sure!" said Sarah Jo. "That is, unless it's like the proverbial phoenix and rises out of the ashes." They both laughed at that. It had been a crazy year – one of surprises, some not so good. But now things seemed to be leveling off, at least from Sarah Jo's perspective. The future would surely hold better things!

***

Sarah Jo and Luke, and Callie and Austin made quite the dashing foursome the night of the formal. Sarah Jo felt like a princess in her new waltz length pale yellow gown. Luke commented that she looked stunning; she couldn't remember ever being called that. Callie, as well, had made an impression on home schoolers and public school students alike. Although it was unspoken, those in the public schools secretly wondered if the home school students would measure up, especially since this was a public school sponsored event. Those who were home schooled were eyed with a bit of suspicion as if they were not quite up to the standard of public school students. But that night nobody made harsh comparisons, judging by the looks of things. All were having fun.

"Well," said Luke, "do you want to try for having something to eat before the night is over?" Sarah Jo remembered the horrible experience that happened last time, after the Homecoming dance.

"Sure, why not?" said Sarah Jo confidently. "Like I've said, when does lightning strike twice?"

"Careful, Sarah Jo. It actually *does* happen," said Austin.

"Tonight it won't," assured Callie. "I just said a prayer."

"Hey, why didn't *I* think of that?

"You will in time, Austin. It becomes second nature," said Callie. The foursome decided that they'd eat at a little mom and pop restaurant in town, something that was a step or two up from a fast food place like they did after the Homecoming dance. This particular restaurant made an effort to extend its hours so that young people – or older ones for that matter – could go there for a bite to eat after the dance. There were a few couples there when they came in, and an older man at the counter nursing along a cup of coffee. Sarah Jo noticed his hands shaking as he put the thick white cup up to his lips. The four found a small table out of the traffic, such as there was. She supposed that it was just the husband and wife holding down the fort; he the cook, and she the waitress.

"This place is fancy," said Callie. "I like the tablecloths on the tables here."

"As opposed to?" asked Luke.

"As opposed to someone making a piggy mess on the bare table for the next customer to sit at."

"Don't they wipe down the tables afterward?" asked Austin.

"Probably not if they're busy or in a hurry," replied Callie.

"Yeh, or you get the smell of some sort of disinfectant, right?" chimed in Sarah Jo. She opened her menu. The others followed suit.

"What looks good here?" asked Luke. Then, answering his own question he added, "Ah, I see something that's a real palate pleaser."

"You sound like a commercial," said Callie.

"Well, it maybe *will* be if it's as good as I remember it being. I think I'm going to order the chicken fried steak." Luke put his menu down. "What are you having, Austin?"

"I think I'll try the same. It's kinda funny. Back when we were in FLF uh, Future Life Fellowship, we didn't eat a whole lot of meat and stuff. At least they didn't encourage it."

"That's right," said Callie. "I remember how Fern Samuels kind of made an issue of it when I was at the grocery store picking up a few things for Mom for dinner."

"Hey, let's forget about her," said Sarah Jo. "This has been a fun night so far. Let's keep it that way, okay?" Soon they had all made their choices and the waitress took their orders. Sarah Jo decided on a fajita, and Callie on a Chinese sampler.

Later on, as Sarah Jo looked back on it as she waited for sleep to come, nestled in her warm bed, she thought life couldn't be more perfect. Her future looked bright with college starting in the fall and with Luke in her life as a good friend – and that didn't count Callie and Austin and even Abby although she didn't hear from her very often. Her mother kept her busy with her studies and chores, but Sarah Jo still liked her as a friend.

***

Sarah Jo woke up to birds chirping outside her window even though it was closed. Robins had already been spotted around town. After a long winter, those kinds of things usually ended up on the front page of the paper, even if in rather obscure places. She turned over in her bed, thinking she might capture another fifteen minutes of sleep; that wasn't meant to be. Her mother called up the stairs to her and she answered promptly, replying she'd be right down. That wasn't Mom's style unless she was really in a hurry, so it was natural for her to wonder why she was being summoned. She dressed and went downstairs.

"What's up, Mom?"

"I need to go to the store and I wondered if you'd keep an eye on the bread in the oven."

"Sure," answered Sarah Jo. "You usually don't shop on Saturday morning though."

"Oh, I need to get some creamer for the coffee, plus I'll pick up a couple other things I need too."

"You want me to go over on the bike?"

"It's okay, dear. I just need you to keep an eye on the bread. I made it and kneaded it in the maker but I decided to put it in a loaf pan, let it rise and then bake it. It should come out in about a half hour."

"Okay Mom, will do." Turned out that watching the bread and taking it out would be the easiest part of the day. Sarah Jo found that out the hard way. Mom had already come back and noticed that the bread looked perfect. As for Sarah Jo, she got a phone call on her own phone and it turned out to be none other than Mrs. Fern Samuels.

"Hello, Sarah Jo?"

"Yes, who's calling, please?

"This is Fern Samuels. You remember me, don't you?" Sarah Jo certainly did, but she didn't know why she'd be calling. "I tried calling your friend Callie, but there was no answer. Then I thought better of it and decided to call you."

"What is this about, Mrs. Samuels? I don't believe we have anything to talk about."

"Well, actually we do, Sarah Jo. May I please tell you the reason for this call?"

"Actually, you caught me at kind of a bad time-"

"I called *you* because it has to do with Austin and I figured your friend Callie might spill the beans, as they say, to Austin. It's actually about a surprise graduation party for him," said Fern Samuels.

"I'm sorry, but I don't think I can be of help."

"How do you know that? I haven't even told you what I have in mind."

"Look, Mrs. Samuels, I usually don't get involved with other people's business. His family probably has something planned for him."

"No," said Mrs. Samuels. "They don't. I would know. We attend the same church."

"W-well," faltered Sarah Jo. "I don't know how this concerns me."

"It does, dear. It most certainly does." 'Dear'? thought Sarah Jo. "I need you, Sarah Jo, to help me organize this."

"Mrs. Samuels, I'm busy with my own end-of-year school activities."

"Yes, but you are in home school. There's a whole lot more flexibility," pushed back Mrs. Samuels.

"I'm quite sure I can't help you, Mrs. Samuels, but I'll call you if I can."

"Why not commit now? I need to know sooner rather than later."

"I said I'll call you if I'm able to help, Mrs. Samuels. Right now I have to go. Good bye." What a persistent woman, thought Sarah Jo. She should've been in sales. Since Callie's continual run-ins with that Samuels woman, she herself had developed a sense of dread of ever being in contact with her and now here she'd been called by her. How had Mrs. Samuels gotten her number? she wondered. She probably had her way; she seemed to know a lot of people. She'd have to tell Callie about this whole thing. She certainly didn't want anything to do with her after all she'd learned from Callie, not to mention the Homecoming dance fiasco.

***

Sarah Jo called Callie that afternoon. Would Callie like to go out for cocoa or something? Callie would, so they decided to meet up for a nice steaming cup of cocoa at Corky's. It wasn't as good as Connie's but for a coffee house they did hot chocolate very well.

Callie got there first, but Sarah Jo arrived soon after. It was still cold enough outside that the warm, if not steamy, atmosphere of Corky's felt great.

"So Sarah Jo, to what do I owe the pleasure of this meeting?"

"What? Talk English, Cal."

"Oh come on, Sarah Jo, I'm just trying to keep things lighthearted. Any time you call and want to meet up it's usually something serious."

"Well, I never expected to hear from Fern Samuels, and here she calls me out of the blue."

"Why would she want to talk to *you*?" Sarah Jo brought the cup of hot cocoa to her lips and took a sip.

"Well, that's the other thing, Cal. She didn't want you to know about it. I had suggested she call you."

"Sheesh! Thanks a lot!" returned Callie. "Really, I *do* mean it. I don't need her meddling in Austin's life - and neither does he."

"Well, that's why I tried to downplay it with her. I wanted to get off the phone, so I told her I had to get going."

"It's sad," said Callie, "that you have to treat some people that way. They just don't take a hint."

"That's for sure!"

"So, what are you going to do about it, SJ?"

"Nothing really."

"Wow! You're brave, standing up to Fern Samuels."

"She won't bother me, Cal. I've got friends in high places – I'll be praying. You can too."

"You can count on it!" The two finished their cocoa and went out into the early spring afternoon.

***

Later that evening Sarah Jo thought about Fern Samuels. Why was she so annoying? It didn't take a genius to figure out how she'd messed up Callie's life, let alone Austin's. Of course Mrs. Samuels didn't belong to a *real* church anyway. She'd learned enough from Callie's research to know that was true. They were way off base in what they believed, especially when it came to replacing Jesus with a man. Mrs. Samuels persisted in staying in Future Life Fellowship even though she'd heard the truth about it. I guess that was what Callie referred to as cult mind control. They say that there are none so blind as those who just won't see – they refuse to acknowledge the facts even if they are shown to them.

Chapter Twenty

Anyone who thought high school graduation for a home schooled student was ho-hum would do well to think twice, thought Sarah Jo. It's a *really* big deal. The home schooling community knew that as well and the parents were planning a group graduation. It was to be held at a Pine Moor city park and would make use of the gazebo near the center. Needless to say, Sarah Jo was excited; in fact, it was an understatement. Since so many students would have relatives in attendance, there would be a need for many folding chairs. Those would be set up on the morning of graduation exercises. Students were invited to help and then return at three o'clock that afternoon.

She reminded herself that she needed to order her cap and gown; that couldn't wait any longer. Although it would arrive by next week, she dare not put it off a moment longer. She looked forward to donning the long-waited garment and its matching cap for many years. She just hoped it wouldn't be a rogue sweltering hot day that sometimes comes along in June. Oh well, she would wear a very summery dress underneath her gown. In fact, some girls even wore shorts and a sleeveless blouse. That might be very impractical if they were to go out to dinner or a celebration. Her light, soft pink floral lawn summer dress would work just fine. It was practically new.

Sarah Jo's phone audibly notified her of a text. Hmmm, I don't recognize the number, she thought. It wasn't long before she recognized who'd sent it. It said in upper case letters: CONGRATULATIONS! Fern Samuels

She should have guessed it might be her, but at least that woman owned the text she'd sent. Why did Mrs. Samuels have to be involved in the events in her life – especially the important ones? Apparently, this would be no different. It seemed that she had made herself plenty clear to Mrs. Samuels, but that woman didn't get the message – or chose not to. After that call she'd gotten from her regarding a graduation party for Austin, anything might be possible. Sarah Jo concluded that, simply stated, Mrs. Samuels was a plain old troublemaker. The Bible doesn't hold those who sow discord in very high esteem, thought Sarah Jo, so it was evident that Mrs. Samuels and her so-called church didn't have an accurate version of the Bible. She wanted to steer clear of that woman and planned to do so, even if it meant blocking her number.

Sarah Jo looked out her bedroom window as she sat on her bed. She noticed one stubborn now-faded autumn leaf that clung stubbornly to a branch. It was a couple months since Spring had arrived and it would soon be time for the trees to begin renewing their leaves for the season. Yet there was that lone leaf fluttering in the breeze. A thought occurred to Sarah Jo. What if Mrs. Samuels was like that leaf – tenacious and unyielding? Maybe the "spirit" of that game Spin and Win – or Not! was clinging to her like an infection, eating away at her sensibilities? Perhaps she would have been a different person had she rejected the powers that it had. But for that to be so, it would have taken knowledge of such a power or spirit. Why didn't their so-called church teach that?

So, how would she answer Mrs. Samuels' text? Easy – she wouldn't. She had nothing to say to her – unless it would be "preach speech" and she didn't believe in that. No, and she couldn't even afford to say thank you and be polite as she had been taught. Too risky. What she *could* do is continue to pray for her and hope that the Holy Spirit might break through to Mrs. Samuels' deadbolt-locked mind. She only had to be willing to let some Light in, but that was up to that woman. Right now Sarah Jo had more pressing things to consider. After all, her graduation was a once in a lifetime event and she wanted it to be memorable. It represented years of hard work that now had come to fruition in the form of a well-deserved ceremony.

***

That next Sunday at church, Pastor Martin announced that he would like to see all the graduating seniors after the service. Luke was now attending regularly, so that included him as well. The sermon that Sunday was unusually good, to Sarah Jo's way of thinking. It was about how one might spend the rest of his or her life, regardless of age. After Pastor had given his blessing over the congregation at the end, the high school seniors gathered at the back of the church as Pastor shook members' hands as they filed out the door.

"I've told your parents," said Pastor Martin, "that I won't be keeping you long so that they can wait for you in their cars. I just wanted to let you know that you are a very special group of young men and women and you may partake in our graduation service which will be held the Sunday after graduation. I would like you to wear your caps and gowns that day, if you would, please. That way everyone will know who you are. You'll be asked to come to the front of the church for a special blessing. This will be after our first hymn is sung. You may then remain there when we sing a second hymn and then return to your seats. I know your parents will all be very proud of you, just as Mrs. Martin and I are. Are there any questions? Yes, Luke."

"Is this for *all* graduating students?

"Yes, it is. Please, all of you who are new or attend elsewhere, invite your parents and family members to our service. We will have finger foods and beverages downstairs after the service is concluded. This has all been taken care of by our hospitality committee so there's no need to bring anything." Pastor Martin waited for a few seconds and said, "If there are no other questions, you may be on your way."

"I just *love* this church!" declared Callie as she went upstairs. Luke and Austin nodded in agreement.

***

Lunchtime at the Foster house was unusually lively. Even Mark joined in the discussion that just happened to do with graduation.

"Do you think our church will honor *me* when I'm a senior?" he asked as he stuffed a forkful of chili into his mouth.

"Mark, please don't talk with your mouth full," reproved Mom. "And yes, most likely you too will be honored by our church – *when* you graduate."

"That will be an important day for *you*, Mark," said Sarah Jo.

"Are you trying to tell me something?" he asked.

"Just that you should knuckle down on your studies is all. It pays off."

"And what makes you think I'm not?" asked Mark.

"Are you?"

"Yes, I am, Miss Know-It-All."

"All right, that's enough," boomed Dad. He turned to Mom. "You sure outdid yourself on this chili."

"Thanks, hon."

"So Sarah Jo, how does it feel to be an almost-graduate?" asked Dad.

"I don't really know because I've never been one before," she answered. She hoped he wouldn't think she was being flippant, but the truth was she really *didn't* know.

I realize that, but it's like an adventure, isn't it? I mean really the beginning of your grown up journey."

"That's true, Dad, but it's also a little bit scary. The future is sort of the unknown."

"Yes, Sarah Jo, but you'll be living with us yet for quite some time. You'll get used to your new responsibilities before you actually go out on your own – and even then you'll be living in a dorm at State with a roommate," said Mom.

"You'd better pick a good one," cautioned Mark.

"Well, I don't know if I'll have a choice on that," mumbled Sarah Jo.

***

Time seemed to fly by as Graduation exercises drew near. Sarah Jo,

Callie, Wendy and Laura kept in close touch over the days prior to graduation for each of them. There was a lot to talk about; compare notes etc. Although summer was ahead, they each had to think about summer jobs as well as their plans in the Fall. Callie bemoaned the fact that Austin would be headed out to State, but was comforted by the fact that he was still at an in-state school.

"Just think of it, Cal," said Sarah Jo. "He could have gone to a college far away. Then you wouldn't see him much at all."

"That's true, maybe once or twice a year."

"Now you can see him maybe a couple weekends per month, well, after he gets settled."

"Right. I want to be there for him to support and encourage him spiritually," said Cal. "This will make it easier to do that."

"Your life sure has changed since you accepted Fern Samuels' invitation to her home schooling information session."

"No kidding! Who would've thought I would've gotten to know Austin, let alone see him come out of that Future Life Fellowship."

"Right, Cal. That was a miracle in itself."

Chapter Twenty-One

Finally the day had arrived that home schooled seniors had been waiting for – Graduation! Sarah Jo could hardly wait to receive her diploma. It had been a long way to the finish line, but now she was here. She knew Callie and the others were excited too. The nice thing was that, along with graduating home schooled seniors and their families, friends such as Austin and Luke would be attending too. Sarah Jo was hopeful that maybe Wendy and Laura could make it from Addison, but neither of them were able.

"Make sure someone takes plenty of pictures and video," said Wendy. "I'd be there if I could."

Sarah Jo knew Laura wanted to be there as well, but she had a graduation party to attend of a close friend in Addison.

***

"Sarah Jo, are you just about ready?" asked Mom who called up the stairs.

"Just about. I'm fixing my hair. Give me five minutes."

"Well, you need to get there early. Dad, Mark and I will find our chairs and wait. It's such a lovely day." And it was. The skies were blue, punctuated with puffy white clouds with just a hint of a breeze – enough to allow the fragrance of Spring to be transported gently through the air. The family arrived at Riverview Park. It was beautiful at this time of year, thought Sarah Jo as she made her way to the gazebo. It was decorated with a huge vase of flowers, as well as with greenery. It looked very dignified as suited the occasion, yet welcoming. The graduates took their seats in front of the dais, and the parents and visitors farther back in neat, even rows, on the lawn.

"Mom, why can't we sit in that gazebo thing?" asked Mark.

"It's only for the graduates. They'll be getting up to receive their diplomas up front."

"Doesn't Sarah Jo look excited?" said Mr. Foster to his wife.

"She sure does, dear. It's a big day for her." Mark squirmed in his chair.

"Sit still, son," ordered Dad. "You'll have plenty of time to move around after the ceremony.

***

Sarah Jo tried to remain calm as she waited for her name to be called. It seemed like forever for the Director of Home School Education for their district had covered the Welcome and Introduction as well as a Commencement speech.

"Jared Fisher." He was sitting next to her and got up to receive his diploma. Sarah Jo had seen his name in the Homeschool Newsletter that came once a month.

"Sarah Jo Foster." It was her turn! She got up, being very careful not to catch her deep blue graduation gown on the edge of her chair. She walked up to Mrs. Stewart who handed her the diploma. The mayor of Pine Moor, George Lewis, was also there to shake the graduates' hands.

"Congratulations," Mayor Lewis said as he shook Sarah Jo's hand. She could hardly believe it. She had graduated! She was holding her graduation certificate in her left hand; the proof was there! The graduates gathered in front of the gazebo as they had before the ceremony had started and, with, well wishes from Mrs. Stewart with Mayor Lewis at her side, the grads took their mortarboards and threw them up in the air. Cheers followed. Sarah Jo wanted to keep hers because he had earned the distinction of a gold tassel meaning her academic career had been exceptional. Callie approached her with it.

"Looking for this?" she asked. "Congratulations, Sarah Jo!" Sarah Jo took the square flat mortarboard with the gold tassel.

"Congratulations, Callie!" It was like a family reunion as graduates and their families hugged, shook hands and congratulated the new group of "hope for the future," as Mayor Lewis had put it.

Austin and Luke joined Sarah Jo and Callie with hugs and well-wishing. Then they all headed toward the picnic tables laden with food, contributed by local restaurants. It was a goodwill gesture, not to mention good for business. Fried chicken, fancy hamburgers, potato salad, relishes such as pickles, olives and fresh vegetables whittled into finger-sized munchables were there. Desserts of hand pies, cookies and even doughnuts were available. There were also beverages of hot coffee, tea and ice cold soda as well as milk.

"Can you believe it, Callie?" said Sarah Jo. "We're graduates!"

"I know. It's exciting, isn't it?" The Foster family made their way though the group crowded around the food tables. Mark had accomplished his mission of reaching the tables and loading up on his favorite foods.

"Now *this* is what I'm talking about," he declared, as he bit into a burger; next into a drumstick he'd loaded onto his plate with two more pieces of chicken.

"Let's sit down," said Sarah Jo. "There's an empty table under that tree."

"It seems that the food table is quite a magnet," said Callie. "Everyone's gathered around it.

"Have you got room for two more at this table?" It was Sarah Jo's parents. Austin and Luke got up and Luke said. "We do now."

"Yes," Sarah Jo answered. "Exactly two. Please don't make us watch Mark as he wolfs down his food. That's an appetite crusher for anyone present." Austin and Luke found seating next to the girls.

"He did seem to be ravenous," said Mrs. Foster. "Where *does* he put all that food?"

"He's a future basketball star in the making, just like Luke and Austin," assured Mr. Foster. "Build your body when you're young, right?" Sarah Jo looked at Callie and shrugged as she took a prudent bite from her burger.

"So, Callie, next up is the Graduation service at church. Are you excited?"

"Sort of, but I haven't come down from my high today yet. This was pretty awesome!" Sarah Jo and Luke, Austin and Callie finished and got up from the table; then threw their paper plates into a trash can.

Chapter Twenty-Two

Small groups of people stood outside the church talking on that Graduation Service Sunday. Callie wondered how they'd all fit into the church with that many. Still, as Pastor Martin always said regarding church attendance: Better too many than not enough.

"Hey Cal," greeted Sarah Jo. "Is Austin here yet?"

"Yes, he's here with Luke. Luke's parents are here. I don't know about Austin's."

"He said something about them coming," said Callie. "It would be nice if they did. I think things are pretty well patched up between the three of them.

"Who saw *that* coming?"

"Um, maybe God did. He knows everything."

"Right, Cal. He does."

***

The girls entered the church and sat with the group of graduates being honored. They were dressed in their caps and gowns as Pastor Martin had requested. It was almost as exciting as Graduation itself was. The modest church began filling up with its congregation plus guests. Flowers that decorated the premises filled the air with a light fragrance. The colorful hyacinths seemed to be trying to outdo the other blooms in terms of their aromatic sweet scents. The familiar refrain of a much-loved hymn filled the building, but soon the volume was lessened as Pastor Martin approached the lectern.

"Let us bow our head in prayer. Heavenly Father, today is a special day – one of great hope for the youth of our community. We thank You for each and every one of them. We also ask a special blessing on the sermon today and pray that we glorify You in all that we do. We ask this in Jesus' name. Amen."

"Amen." came the enthusiastic response.

"Let us sing hymn number 65, *We Are His.*" A rustling of pages from the hymnals was followed by the organ's strains of the requested hymn.

"Please be seated," said Pastor Martin. "Today I hope we can all honor our graduates who truly are the hope of tomorrow. Each and every one of them has worked hard for their day of graduation and their future. Never before have we needed such responsible adults as the ones we have here in attendance today. I would like each of them to stand and turn around to face the congregation so that all may see who they are. The grads got up and did as directed, followed by applause from the other occupants of the church.

To Callie's surprise – or shock – latecomers Fern Samuels and daughter Olivia came in, along with Austin's parents, and seated themselves near the front of the church. Sarah Jo sent a questioning look in Callie's direction, to which Callie just shrugged. Their arrival had not gone unnoticed by Pastor Martin.

"Welcome, guests. Today we are honoring our graduates. I'm grateful for all who've come for that purpose. He smiled at those who had just come in. Olivia shifted her position to see who was behind her, while Fern Samuels looked straight ahead as if waiting for a sermon.

Callie glanced at Sarah Jo and thought about how blessed she was to have experienced home school as well as to have good friends of like mind. Sarah Jo was the best. She cherished their friendship.

The morning progressed with a short but meaningful sermon by Pastor Martin. It was followed by a hymn that all – except perhaps Fern Samuels and Austin's parents - knew well.

"Thank you all for coming today and helping celebrate this occasion with our young people," said Pastor Martin. "Let's go downstairs now to Fellowship Hall and enjoy a lunch prepared by some wonderful ladies in our congregation." The group made it downstairs little by little. Callie was surprised to see Mrs. Samuels and Olivia as well as Austin's parents also disappear down the steps. That seemed unusual. Was Mrs. Samuels waiting to talk to Austin in a more informal setting? Callie noticed Austin in the crowd but Mrs. Samuels was not nearby. She and Olivia and Austin's parents were waiting in line to serve themselves at the buffet table. What a variety of food! The smell was incredible too, in Callie's opinion. Pretty soon all were sitting down, except those who'd come back for seconds - to the gaily decorated tables with Spring flowers. There was a buzz of voices and some laughter as well.

At the end of the feasting, Pastor Martin stood up and thanked everyone for coming. He said he felt one last prayer of thanks might be appropriate and proceeded to give one. Suddenly, up popped little Olivia Samuels who ran over to Pastor Martin. She hugged his legs which was all she could reach and declared in a very loud voice, "Mommy, I like this church! I want to come back here again. Everyone is so nice – nicer than the church we go to!"

*****